"Don't sugarcoat it. J........ straight."

"It looks like the guy in your car last night is the TRK serial killer. As far as I'm aware," Nash continued, "TRK didn't send letters to his victims beforehand. Which means a different person, one with a grudge against you, wrote them. Mailing them from different post offices, moving strategically closer could indicate they're preparing to take action. Perhaps to scare you."

"Well, it's working." Lynn exhaled a shaky breath. "I'm downright terrified." Trembling, she wrapped her arms around herself protectively.

If he were working a case, this was where he'd step away, giving the civilian space to emotionally gather themselves. But Lynn needed him.

Nash reached out and brought Lynn close, pressing her to his chest. She shivered harder, burying her face in the crook of his neck and slipping her arms around him. Caressing a hand up and down her back, he vowed to find a way to keep her safe.

"You're going to be okay. I won't let anyone hurt you."

WYOMING WINTER RESCUE

———

JUNO RUSHDAN

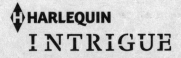

For JBR. Thank you for your unwavering support and love.

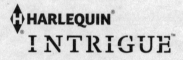

HARLEQUIN INTRIGUE™

Recycling programs
for this product may
not exist in your area.

ISBN-13: 978-1-335-58305-5

Wyoming Winter Rescue

Copyright © 2022 by Juno Rushdan

For questions and comments about the quality of this book,
please contact us at CustomerService@Harlequin.com.

Harlequin Enterprises ULC
22 Adelaide St. West, 41st Floor
Toronto, Ontario M5H 4E3, Canada
www.Harlequin.com

Printed in U.S.A.

Juno Rushdan is the award-winning author of steamy, action-packed romantic thrillers that keep readers on the edge of their seats. She writes about kick-ass heroes and strong heroines fighting for their lives as well as their happily-ever-afters. As a veteran air force intelligence officer, she uses her background supporting Special Forces to craft realistic stories that make readers sweat and swoon. Juno currently lives in the DC area with her patient husband, two rambunctious kids and a spoiled rescue dog. To receive a free book from Juno, sign up for her newsletter at junorushdan.com/mailing-list. Also be sure to follow Juno on BookBub for the latest on sales at bit.ly/bookbubjuno.

Books by Juno Rushdan

Harlequin Intrigue

Cowboy State Lawmen

Wyoming Winter Rescue

Fugitive Heroes: Topaz Unit

Rogue Christmas Operation
Alaskan Christmas Escape
Disavowed in Wyoming
An Operative's Last Stand

A Hard Core Justice Thriller

Hostile Pursuit
Witness Security Breach
High-Priority Asset
Innocent Hostage
Unsuspecting Target

Tracing a Kidnapper

Visit the Author Profile page at Harlequin.com.

CAST OF CHARACTERS

Lynn Delgado—A psychotherapist struggling to hold it together after she begins receiving threatening letters and becomes the target of a killer.

Nash Garner—This FBI agent with a Special Forces background will stop at nothing to keep his ex safe. But as the threat closes in, he realizes that he may have met his match.

Holden Powell—Longtime friend of Nash and chief deputy at the sheriff's department.

Shirley Crombie—An angry mother who has a grudge against Lynn, but is she behind the vicious letters? Or is she up to something much worse?

Yvonne Lamber—She's eager to get out of town with her best friend, Lynn, and help her forget about her troubles.

Chapter One

"Nash, don't bother coming." Lourdes Lynn Delgado cradled her cell phone between her ear and shoulder as she locked her computer screen and grabbed her purse. "There's nothing left to say. Besides, I'm already leaving the office." She should've left an hour ago.

"I'm sorry I'm running late, Lynn."

To her, Lourdes was her grandmother, so almost everyone called Lynn by her middle name, which she preferred since she was the namesake of someone still living. Although her family affectionately called her Lola for as long as she could remember. For some reason, Nash had never taken to it.

"Running late is ten minutes. Not sixty." Nonetheless, here she was with a grumbling stomach at 8:00 p.m., waiting on him. Like an idiot.

"I got hung up at work," Nash said, "and before you say it, *yes*, as usual."

He was an FBI agent, saving lives and stopping bad guys. She admired him for it, but his tardiness only scratched the surface of a much deeper problem in their relationship.

"Wait for me." The entreaty in his voice tugged at her, but she braced against it, refusing to get sucked back in. "I'll be there in five minutes," he said, which she'd learned meant twenty. "Wait, okay? We need to talk."

She didn't believe it. He wasn't going to shed the military stoicism from his former army ranger days any time soon and suddenly open up.

"You haven't changed." Lynn turned off her office lights. "What we need is a clean break."

As a psychotherapist she knew that seeing one another after a breakup while being attracted to each other and still having feelings wasn't advisable. Studies suggested time apart was best. Six months without any interaction. Without speaking on the phone. Without letting the good memories cloud judgment and convince her that separating was a mistake.

Lynn stepped into the hallway. "I'm leaving now." She locked her office door. "Don't come to my house, either. We're done." Saying the words out loud made her heart ache. She'd once envisioned building a life with him, but if they were wrong for each other, it was better to end things now before they got in any deeper. "It's for the best. Good night."

After she disconnected, she put her phone in her purse and turned to leave.

Movement at the end of the hall stopped her cold. The cozy waiting room near the front door was dimly lit by one lamp and the plugged-in glowing jack-o'-lantern on the side table. She hesitated a minute but didn't see anyone, didn't hear anything. With Halloween coming up and all the horror movies she'd been watching, her subconscious was probably playing tricks on her.

Yet the warning hairs on the nape of her neck rose. "Hello."

Maybe it was her colleague, Dr. Richard Jennings, whose practice she had joined last year. Or perhaps one of his clients. She couldn't recall if he'd mentioned any late appointments.

Lynn strode down the hall, treading lightly on the carpet until she could see the entire waiting room and the front door.

She saw something. Or rather someone. Standing in the corner, in the shadows.

A woman?

No…a man. Definitely a man.

"Rich, is that you?" Even as she asked the question, she could now tell it wasn't. The height and build were wrong. Too short, too slim to be Rich.

The man stepped into the light.

It was Andy Crombie. One of her clients she'd been concerned about since their last session.

Lynn tamped down her rising fear. "Andy? What are you doing here? It's very late and we don't have an appointment." She stepped closer. "Is everything okay?"

Shaking his head, he burrowed his hands in his pockets. His shaggy black hair was disheveled, with inky strands clinging to his pale face. His brown eyes were watery, his nose swollen and red, his beard shabby. He was wearing a dirty, stained T-shirt and a ragged jacket.

"No," Andy said, with another sharp shake of his head, his voice hoarse. "Everything's not okay." His hand slipped from his pocket. Metal glinted in the amber light.

He had a gun.

Lynn stiffened, but her mind was racing. She'd gone through a course to prepare for a situation like this. Ninety percent of the scenarios from her training hadn't ended well. That was the reason she had decided to stop treating severe psychological pathologies and hadn't opened a practice alone.

She shifted her stance to an angle, allowing her a glimpse of Rich's office without turning her back on Andy. Rich might still there. If so, the door would be unlocked. She hoped.

It was closer than hers, only a few feet away.

As long as Andy kept the gun lowered, down by his side, she might be able to make it.

Slowly, very slowly, Lynn raised her palms. "Stay calm." Her tone was steady and soft despite the fact that her nerves were pinging. "Whatever the problem is, we can find a solution. We can get through this. Together." She crept backward, inch by inch. "But having a gun pointed at me makes me very uncomfortable. Can you put the gun away so we can work through this peacefully?"

He rubbed the side of his face and yanked at his hair. "No."

A knot of tension tightened in her stomach. "Okay, okay. How about putting the gun on the floor or the side table next to you so no one gets hurt by accident."

"I said no," he spat through gritted teeth.

Lynn drew in a strained breath. "Then talk to me. Tell me what the problem is."

"The problem is you." Andy lifted the automatic weapon.

Lynn's heart dropped as a sickening dread washed over her. She stared at the muzzle of the gun.

Silver.

Lethal.

Aimed dead center at her chest.

A scream started in the back of her throat, but Rich wouldn't be able to hear her. The therapy rooms were soundproofed to safeguard the privacy of their clients. As well as to keep outside noise from disrupting a patient's train of thought.

Lynn swallowed back any useless cries for help. "You don't want to hurt me." She took another small step. Another and another. "You don't want to hurt anyone."

"But I do. I really do," he said, jabbing the gun in her direction. "I want to hurt you, the way you hurt me."

Heart thudding, she licked her lips. *Don't panic. Do not panic!* "What's wrong, Andy?"

His gaze roamed while he pinched his lips together. Tears welled in his eyes. The gun shook in his hand. But he didn't answer.

"Please tell me what's wrong." Lynn eased her back up to the door. "I want to help you." She reached for the knob.

"Liar." Andy's gaze flickered up and homed in on her. "It's all your fault." He cocked the hammer of the gun.

Oh, no.

Lynn twisted the doorknob, hopeful it was unlocked.

The cool metal in her hand turned, and scant relief whispered through her. She ducked inside the office, closed the door and engaged the lock.

Spinning around, she faced Rich and his client, Cindy Morris.

Rich's hand fell from Cindy's cheek, and the two of them jumped apart on the sofa like a couple of teenagers caught making out.

Wide-eyed and flushed, Rich hopped to his feet. "Sorry. Uh, I thought you'd already left. We were just, uh…"

Lynn glanced past Cindy, who lowered her head and was adjusting her blouse, and she hustled around behind Rich's desk. She pressed the red panic button that would notify the police. Both offices had one in case of emergencies.

"What are you doing in here?" Rich asked, his tone sliding from apologetic to indignant. "How dare you barge in on a counseling session."

"Andy Crombie is here."

"At this hour?" Rich's puffed-up chest deflated, and he rubbed his trim powder-white beard. For a man in his late fifties, he looked a decade older. "I thought you decided to stop seeing him and referred him to a different therapist."

"He's got a gun."

"What?" Rich blanched.

Cindy bolted up from the sofa and ran to him. The young woman, half his age, grabbed Rich's arm and clung to his side. "Do you think it's loaded?"

Lynn grimaced at the question. "I didn't ask." The odds weren't in their favor. When did anyone in the Cowboy State deliberately carry an *unloaded* firearm?

A gunshot cracked, blasting a hole in the door as bullet-split wood fractured the air.

Cindy shrieked.

Rich dragged her behind the desk beside Lynn, where the three of them huddled together.

The cops would be there soon. They had to be. And Nash was on the way.

Where was he?

Then she remembered their conversation. Telling him not to come because it was pointless.

She gritted her teeth in bitter regret.

Two more rounds were fired into the wood jamb.

"He's going to make it inside before the police

get here," Rich said. "We've got to buy time, do anything to stall him, so he doesn't kill us all."

Time was something they didn't have. It would take the sheriff's department seven to ten minutes to respond.

Another bullet hit the metal doorknob. The shrill sound echoed through Lynn, reverberating down to her bones.

The guts of the latch rattled when Andy kicked the door. On a second kick, the frame splintered, and the door burst open.

Andy stormed inside the office, brandishing the weapon. "You're a liar! If you wanted to help me, you wouldn't have gotten rid of me!" He swung the gun in Lynn's direction.

She cringed, her spine pressed to the wall, grabbing her purse tight against her stomach. Through the soft leather of her handbag, she felt the hard outline of the Ruger LCR .38 revolver that Nash had given her.

The compact gun was simple to operate. She didn't have to think about anything, not even racking a slide. There was no safety, and it had a hammerless design. She'd regarded it as a hazard that could do more harm than good, but when her FBI agent boyfriend prodded her to carry it, she hadn't argued. But she doubted she could ever bring herself to use it.

"Why did you pawn me off on that psychiatrist?" Andy asked, drawing closer.

"I'm sorry." Tightening her grip on her purse with one hand, Lynn slid the other inside. "You need specialized treatment. I thought with his expertise that he'd be a better match for you."

"A better match?" Andy's voice was a fierce whisper. "I thought you cared about me."

"I do." Lynn nodded as her fingers skimmed the cold steel of the Ruger. "Very much." She gripped the handle. "I'm deeply invested in all my clients." It was true. She had struggled with the referral, worried it might affect the progress that had been made. She didn't want him to feel emotionally stranded. And right now, Andy needed her help more than ever. She let go of the gun. They just had to buy time. "I only want what's best for you."

"Liar!" Andy's face twisted in anger. The gun shook in his hand as he leveled it at her chest. "I hate you for lying."

This wasn't happening. Not to her.

"She isn't lying," Rich said. "Don't blame Dr. Delgado. No one is to blame." He stepped forward with his hands at his sides, palms facing forward in a nonthreatening manner.

Cindy clawed at Rich's sleeve, urging him not to move any farther. "What are you doing?" she asked in a frantic whisper, staying behind him. "Don't be a hero."

"It wasn't an easy decision for Dr. Delgado," Rich said. "She consulted me about your case. There were many factors to take into consideration. Her top concern was always your well-being. I advised her to refer you to—"

Pivoting, Andy swung the gun at Rich and pulled the trigger.

The gunshot was like a thunderclap in Lynn's soul. Her knees buckled, and she fell to the floor.

Time slowed. It was as if everything was happening at a distance. Someone else's living nightmare that she was being forced to watch.

Rich was writhing on the carpet, gasping for air. Blood pooled on the carpet beside him.

Screaming, Cindy dropped to her knees, lowered her face to the floor and covered her head with her hands.

Everything inside Lynn went numb. She was disconnected, reeling in disbelief.

Rich's legs stopped twitching. He was no longer moving.

Oh God. Is he dead?

"I was warned not to trust you," Andy said. "I should've listened." He stalked around the desk.

Lynn couldn't breathe, couldn't think. She looked up, her gaze not making it to his face, locked on the sight of the pistol in his hand. Pressure built in her chest. Her ears filled with the roar of white noise as Andy lowered the gun, pointing it straight at her head.

Chapter Two

It was his lucky night.

Nash Garner pulled his truck into the parking lot across the street from the small one-story clinic. Lynn's SUV was still there, along with three other vehicles. He hadn't missed her. After a horrendous week at work, finally something was going his way. She must've decided to wait five extra minutes. Not that it had taken him that long. He'd made it in four, but it wouldn't smooth over the fact he was an hour late.

On top of that, he had to convince Lynn to give him another chance. He was usually the one to bail on a casual fling after a couple of months. Figures, this was the first *relationship* he wanted to last, and he was the one getting kicked to the curb.

Second time was the charm. At least for him. He'd failed ranger school on the first try, but he hadn't given up and had gotten in on his next attempt. Same with the FBI. He'd neglected to properly study for the initial exam. A miscalculation he didn't repeat. Getting things right the first time wasn't his forte, but he was a quick learner and never made the same mistake twice.

He hopped out of his truck and headed across the street. Then he remembered the flowers sitting on the passenger seat that he'd picked up to help lower Lynn's defenses. Going back to get the bouquet of camellias and roses, her favorites, he decided he wasn't going to leave the clinic until they had talked, again. The first time, he'd listened, mumbled a bit and shut down.

This time would be different. No matter how long it took, and it might be a while considering he had no idea where to begin, he was going to put his all into trying.

He clutched the door handle of his truck, the sight of the flowers on the seat making him smile.

Gunshots rang out, piercing his thoughts. Three in close succession.

They had come from inside the clinic.

Adrenaline sparked inside him. Dashing across the street, he whipped out his cell phone and dialed 911.

The line rang. An operator answered. "Laramie 911, police, fire and—?"

"This is Special Agent Nash Garner. Shots fired at the Turning Point clinic," he said, reaching the entrance. He couldn't see inside, because the glass of the front door was tinted. "I need backup now."

A fourth shot was fired.

Without waiting for a response from the operator, he hung up, drew his sidearm from his holster and swept inside in the building.

After a quick scan of the waiting room, he cleared it.

Light spilled out from the first office. Voices carried down the hall: Lynn's, a man's—one he didn't recognize—and Rich's.

Another shot boomed.

A scream punctured the air.

Nash's heartbeat kicked up a fraction. Everything around him sharpened, his senses going into battle mode. He moved on silent feet down the hall until he reached Rich's office.

He took in the busted side jamb and bullet holes in the door.

From the hall, his gaze landed on Rich, on the floor, wounded. Not moving. A woman was screaming. She was crouched in a corner, head pressed to the floor near Rich's feet.

Not Lynn.

"I was warned not to trust you. I should've listened," said a man, who was out of his line of sight.

Easing inside the office with his weapon at the ready, Nash spotted the man holding a gun. The guy stood on the other side of the desk, his back to the shrieking blonde, his focus on somebody else. His weapon was pointed at the individual hidden from Nash's view by the desk.

It could only be one person. Lynn.

His training usually kicked in without hesitation, but for a frozen heartbeat, Nash feared Lynn was a dead woman. The nanosecond ticked on.

Everything happened all at once, bleeding together.

Weapon trained on the gunman, the words rose in his throat—*FBI, drop your gun*—but not fast enough. Nash got out the first syllable. "Eff—"

The man's gaze whipped to him as another gunshot exploded in the room.

The guy jerked backward. A red stain blossomed on his chest, center mass. His weapon fell from his hands, and he slumped to the floor in a crumpled heap.

Relief flooded Nash along with regret. Lynn was alive. She had been his main concern. But she'd killed someone because he'd been seconds too late.

Nash raced around the desk. Lynn was sitting on her heels, still as stone, arm still raised, hand concealed inside her purse. Wisps of smoke rose from a hole in the leather.

"Lynn, are you okay?" He kicked the perpetrator's weapon away and holstered his own.

She didn't move, didn't look at him. Only stared at the space where the gunman had stood. She didn't even seem to be breathing.

Nash knelt in front of her. "Lynn." He brushed her long, dark brown hair from her face and put a gentle hand on her shoulder. Her olive skin was pale, almost ashen, her lips pinched until they were colorless. Her amber eyes, usually so full of life, were glazed and dull. "Lynn," he said again, this time giving her a slight shake.

Drawing in a sudden breath, she blinked. Briefly her gaze was lost as if coming out of a trance, then realization chased off the expression. She looked at him, and her raised arm began to shake.

"Are you hurt?" He slowly took the purse from around her hand and put it on the floor. Then he pried the gun from her trembling fingers.

"Y-y-you shot him." She looked down at the man who had threatened her life but quickly shuddered and glanced away back to Nash.

"No," he said, shaking his head. "I didn't. You did." The trauma of what'd happened must've been too much for her. Nash looked over at the dead body. He could only begin to imagine what she and the other two had gone through.

"Me?" A sob caught in her throat.

"You did what you had to do." She must have acted on pure instinct. "It's going to be okay." He glanced back at her. "I need to check on the others. All right?"

She gave a weak nod.

Nash hurried over to Rich and put two fingers to his carotid artery in his neck. There was a pulse. A strong one. The wound was in his shoulder. He was probably in shock, but it was also possible a main artery had been hit and he was bleeding out. Nash grabbed a handkerchief from the inner pocket of his blazer and applied pressure to the gunshot wound to slow the bleeding.

He glanced at the woman, who was now sobbing as she rocked back and forth with her arms wrapped around herself. "Hey, what's your name?"

"Cindy. Cindy Morris."

Despite the screaming and crying, she looked to be in better shape than Lynn. "Are you injured?"

"No. But Rich. Oh God. You have to help him."

Nash was doing his best to stanch the blood flow.

Two men swept into the office, wearing black uniforms, weapons at the ready. Nash hadn't heard any sirens. If Rich or Lynn had triggered the silent alarm earlier, then it was law enforcement's protocol to approach without alerting the offender that they were on the scene.

"Sheriff." Nash tipped his head at Daniel Clark. They were well acquainted. Not only from working cases, but his best friend was the chief deputy. Nash was known to pop into the office for professional as well as personal reasons.

"An ambulance is on the way," Daniel said, surveying the room while the other deputy went to check on the women and verify the culprit was dead. He pulled down the radio attached to his shoulder and notified the EMTs en route of the gunshot wound. "What happened here?" He took out a notepad and pen.

Nash gave a quick rundown of what little he knew, with one modification. He neglected to mention that the assailant had acknowledged him with a look, even though his head had been in motion, and he'd kept his weapon pointed at Lynn. This was a case of self-defense. The gunman had already shot one person. Nash didn't want to say anything that might cast a shadow of the slightest doubt on the situation, or on Lynn. He'd do anything to protect her. Cindy's head had been down, making it unlikely she'd say anything to contradict his version of events, and Lynn was too confused to say something that might hurt herself.

The thought of how close he had come to losing her burned his gut.

"Rich has a strong pulse," Nash said. "If there aren't any internal complications, he should pull through. Lynn and Cindy will have to fill you in on what led up to all this."

Two EMTs hustled into the room, carrying a medical bag and a stretcher. Once they signaled to Nash that he could take pressure off the wound, he stood and moved out of their way. The techs worked quickly, but thoroughly, patching up the gunshot wound, transferring Rich to the stretcher and getting him out of the building.

That could've been Lynn. Injured and bleeding, being rushed to the hospital. The other alternative, her in a body bag, was something he couldn't bear.

"Just to be clear," Daniel said to Nash, "after

you identified yourself, the assailant didn't drop his weapon?"

"Everything happened fast, almost simultaneously. I was in the process of identifying myself." Then he would've told the man to stop and throw down his weapon. None of which he'd had the chance to get out of his mouth, because it had all gone to hell in a handbasket. "But he didn't drop his weapon until after Lynn shot him."

"Bag up the gun that was used," Daniel said to the deputy.

"Already done," the deputy responded, wearing gloves and holding up an evidence bag.

"Once we officially close the case, we'll return it to Lynn," Daniel said. "Should be a day or two if everything checks out." He perused his notes and gave a low whistle. "They all got pretty lucky. Provided Dr. Jennings pulls through."

Across the room, the deputy finished taking Cindy's statement.

"She saved us," Cindy said, tears streaming down her cheeks. "He was going to kill her and then he probably would've killed me, too."

The deputy patted Cindy on the back. "Okay. Try to calm down." He turned to Lynn and helped her up into Rich's chair.

She was still out of it, suffering from a different kind of shock. Nash wanted to go to her, be at her side, hold her hand through this.

"You should probably go get cleaned up first," Daniel said, as if reading his mind.

Nash's gaze dropped to his bloody palms. "I'll be right back. Would you mind getting Lynn a water, or…" His voice trailed off as he returned his attention to Lynn.

She was in desperate need of something. He doubted water would cut it, but it would be a start.

"Sure." He tipped the edge of his felt cattleman hat up with a knuckle. It wasn't often he wore the cowboy hat in uniform. He gave his deputies the option of wearing one or a ball cap with a sheriff's logo, and he usually sported the latter. "I'll look after her. Go on."

Most folks were aware they'd been a couple since last year. Law enforcement looked out for everyone, but they took special care of their own and by extension loved ones.

His last glimpse as he walked out of the office was Lynn trembling all over while she gave her statement, explaining how she'd found Andy lurking in the waiting room.

Nash strode down the hall, passing Lynn's office. In the bathroom, he scrubbed his hands twice with soap and warm water. His only thought was getting back to her as quickly as possible. She was going to need help through this. Not answering questions about what happened. That part would be fine.

But what would come later, processing everything, coming to terms with it, that would be tough. Especially for someone like Lynn who felt deeply about everything and everyone.

He made his way back to Rich's office. Lynn was holding a glass of amber liquid. There was a half-full bottle of liquor on the desk.

"I didn't hear Nash announce himself." Lynn sipped from the glass and winced as she swallowed. "Like I told you, it was like static in my ears. I didn't hear the Ruger either." Anxiety tightened her voice.

Not wanting to disturb her train of thought, Nash approached slowly.

"I found Jennings's scotch in the desk." Daniel stepped aside to make room for him to get by. "Figured she needed something stronger than water."

Nash clasped his shoulder as a *thank you*. He crouched beside Lynn, taking her free hand between his.

Almost as a reflex, she pulled away from his touch and pressed her palm to her stomach like she was fighting the urge to retch.

Crowding her, making her uncomfortable, wasn't his intent. He didn't want to take her withdrawal personally and even worse, he hated the helpless feeling crawling over him.

Daniel motioned for Nash to move to the side of the room with him and leaned in. "This sort of thing, killing someone, hits everyone differently. For us," he said, gesturing between the two of them, "it's one thing, a possibility that comes with the job. Still…" Daniel blew out a slow, deep breath.

Nodding, Nash understood what hadn't been said because there wasn't a need. Taking someone's life, regardless of the circumstances, was never easy. He'd know.

It took a toll on law enforcement, too. Just a different kind.

"Civilians have no idea what we face, what we have to go through," Daniel continued, his brown skin pulling taut over the sharp slashes of his cheekbones. "But for them, this type of experience can be significantly harder to deal with."

Once again, Nash nodded. Lynn's world had flipped upside down tonight. Although she had defended herself and survived without any visible wounds, of course she would need to heal from this ordeal. "Yeah, I suppose you're right."

"When she's ready to be held and to talk, she'll let you know. Until then, be patient. She might need a little space."

It was sound advice.

Patience he had in spades. Space he could give. Anything Lynn needed, he'd do for her.

No problem.

Chapter Three

Five weeks later

Drumming fingers on the table was the only sound in the room. The cursor flashed on the blank laptop screen. A cold, dark fury swelled, a storm building inside that would be unleashed.

Soon.

Very soon.

This letter had to be short. Concise but clever. To the point but at the same time puzzling. In case the police ever read it, they'd have nothing to go on.

This one had to be the best, standing out from all the other letters.

At last, it became clear what needed to be written.

Tense fingers clacked out the message with enraged strokes of the keys. Taunting words that concealed the bitter anger behind them exploded across the page in all caps.

Once finished, the lines were centered, the fonts and sizes varied to emphasize certain words. Everything was highlighted in bold.

It had taken an hour to think of the right thing to say, seconds to type.

With one final keystroke, the printer hummed,

warming up. The paper chugged and spewed out onto the table. Latex snapped and crackled as gloves were pulled on. There'd be no clues that could be traced back. Only then was the page picked up. After one final check, it was ready to go.

Perfection. This would do the trick.

That woman brought this on herself and deserved what was coming.

The paper was folded with precision, ensuring even, sharp lines, and then stuffed into an envelope that had been stamped and addressed:

Dr. Lynn Delgado
Turning Point Therapy and Wellness Clinic
Laramie, Wyoming

This would be the last letter sent to the high and mighty doctor, but this was far from over. This wouldn't end until Lynn Delgado was no longer breathing.

NASH SLOWED HIS truck in front of the Underground Self-Defense school on Third Street, catching a glimpse of Lynn inside. The sight of her had his heart melting in his chest.

He could stare at her all day. It was the same every time he saw her, which hadn't been much recently.

What he wouldn't give for her to answer one of his calls.

What he wouldn't give to talk to her.

She was in pain, suffering from what had happened with Andrew Crombie. Although she wouldn't admit it, he sensed that she was in trouble. Trapped in a personal hell of her own making.

He could help her through it. If only she'd let him, trust him.

Right after the shooting, she'd taken off to Fort Collins, where she had family, and had refused to take his calls. He had to hear from someone else when she came back to Laramie a month ago.

Then he'd waited, kept giving her space, thinking sooner or later she had to talk to him.

At this point, his patience was threadbare and on the brink of snapping.

A car honked behind Nash.

With a rueful shake of his head, he held up an apologetic hand in his rearview mirror to the inconvenienced driver. He pulled off but decided to circle the block. If he lingered long enough, he'd be able to nab one of the few parking spots on Third Street near the USD school.

After working sixteen hours, he was exhausted and wanted nothing more than to eat dinner and crash, but now that he'd seen Lynn, she was all he could think about.

For some reason, she had been avoiding him,

but this torment of dodge and evade that she was putting them both through had gone on long enough.

Lʏɴɴ ɴᴇᴇᴅᴇᴅ ᴛʜɪs. Bᴀᴅʟʏ.

She parried the incoming blow from her opponent. Then countering, she struck back with a vertical hit at his shoulder. The punch connected, but it didn't slow him down. He attacked with a quick thrust to her midsection that knocked the wind from her lungs, and she fell onto her backside.

He lunged and was on top of her with his hands around her throat. Lynn grabbed his forearms, struggling to break free of his hold.

"Stop," said Charlotte Sharp, the owner and main instructor at USD, Underground Self-Defense.

Her cousin, Rocco, released Lynn's throat and stood.

"Stay down on the mat, Lynn." Charlie turned to the other ladies standing in a circle around the edge of the mat. "What did she do wrong?"

After a long, awkward moment, the only person to raise their hand was Becca Hammond. FBI agent extraordinaire, according to Nash.

Charlie sighed. "Anyone else?" She looked around, but there were no other volunteers. "All right, share with the group."

Becca lit up like a star pupil who had all the

answers. "She never should've let him get on top of her."

"Exactly." Charlie nodded and took a knee beside Lynn. "How do you feel being down here on the mat?"

Lynn shrugged. "I don't know."

"We don't lie to each other," Charlie said. "At least, not in here. How do you feel?"

The same as she did that fateful night in Rich's office when she was down on the floor, cowering, cornered, certain she was going to die. "Weak. Helpless," Lynn admitted.

"Believe it or not," Charlie said, "in a fight, this is the best position for you to be in. Your most powerful weapon is your legs. Next time, use them like we've practiced." Charlie looked around at the group. "You all know what to do."

Charlie was a thorough instructor who had run them through countless drills, but when the moment came and Rocco had lunged, Lynn had failed to do the right thing. Again.

"I reacted," Lynn said. "I didn't think."

"Fear is natural, but don't let it stop you from thinking." Charlie gave her a hard glance but put a supportive hand on her shoulder. "If you do, you won't survive. ATOB, ladies." Always Think Outside the Box. "That's why you're here. To learn, to practice until these self-defense moves become instinctive. Until ATOB becomes instinctive. We're out of time tonight, but Rocco will be back next week. I'll have him come at you again, Lynn. When he does, I want you to kick him with all your strength. Don't forget to vocalize, to harness your power."

"But I might hurt him," Lynn said, not wanting to injure anyone.

"Don't worry about me." Rocco folded his buff arms across his solid chest. "I can handle it."

There was no doubt in Lynn's mind that he could handle himself. The Alcohol, Tobacco and Firearms agent worked on the same joint task force as Nash and Becca. So far, he'd participated in three of the eight women's self-defense classes she'd taken. Charlie wanted the ladies to have a feel for what it was like to go up against a man in a practical scenario.

Lynn climbed to her feet and tugged down her sweatshirt. "When will we learn how to disarm someone who's holding a gun?"

Rocco arched an eyebrow. "Wow, someone wants to sprint ahead a few classes."

"That'll come *much* later." Charlie propped her fists on her slim hips. "First, I need to make sure you have a solid foundation with the basics. My goal is to prepare you to survive. Not endanger any of you. Got it?"

"Yep." Lynn got it, even if she didn't like it.

Charlie put an arm around her shoulder and guided her away from the group. "Are you okay?"

"Sure, sure, I'm fine," Lynn said. She was living a lie. Telling everyone she was fine and that she was coping when in reality she was slowly unraveling. Part of her was embarrassed. She was the trained professional who was supposed to have the answers, but for the first time, she was lost.

"What's up?" Charlie asked. "Is this about those threatening letters you've been getting?"

Lynn made a noncommittal gesture. The truth was, *no* and *yes*.

She'd come here to learn how to protect herself without needing a weapon. For her, the point of this was to survive without anyone losing their life.

"I received another one today," Lynn said. It had been delivered with the late-afternoon mail before she left the office.

"Have you taken them to the sheriff's office?" Charlie asked.

Going to the sheriff meant the chief deputy, who happened to be Nash's best friend, would also know. One quick phone call to Nash, and her ex would know, too.

No, thanks. Anything that would drag Nash back into her mess of a life wasn't a viable option. She thought about him all the time, which only brought her pain. She needed the full six months of no contact to flush him out of her system. Based on the numerous voice mail messages that he'd left for her, he needed the time apart as well to move on.

"I went to the Laramie police," Lynn said. The situation fell in the sheriff's jurisdiction, but the female police chief was willing to advise her. "I was told that law enforcement couldn't do anything about it since the letters are more ominous than outright threatening and couldn't be traced. Once someone acted on them, then the police or the sheriff would be able to do something."

Waiting for someone to try to hurt her sounded far too late in Lynn's opinion.

"Don't worry," Charlie said. "Whoever is sending those letters is a sick coward, only looking to scare you. But it's my job to prepare you just in case. Okay?"

Lynn nodded, though her stomach roiled. If scaring her was their objective, mission accomplished. Those letters had her on edge day and night, living in a perpetual state of anxiety and fear. Thinking about the haunting words had goose bumps prickling her skin.

"I'll see you next time," Charlie said, walking away. "Try to have a good night."

She'd try. Inevitably, she'd also fail.

Swallowing her disappointment at not having mastered the skills she needed to learn, Lynn grabbed her coat, purse and gym bag.

Her body was sore from the workout and her soul leaden. Guilt clung to her, weighing her down like sandbags. Nothing lightened the load, not jogging, not a glass of wine, not a pint of gooey ice cream, not a hot bath. Nothing, except these classes. Even then, they only helped a little.

"Hold on." Becca came up to her. "If you want extra practice," she said, and then lowered her voice, "*free of charge*, I'd be happy to help you on my days off."

That was a generous offer. Unfortunately, Lynn questioned the motivation behind it. "Thanks, but I'll get the hang of it eventually. Can I ask you something?"

"Sure." Becca flashed a bright smile. With her auburn curls pulled back in a ponytail, makeup-free skin showing a dusting of freckles across her face, she looked devoid of ulterior motives, but Lynn knew firsthand that looks could be deceiving. "Ask me anything."

"Why do you come here? You're obviously proficient at this and don't need the classes." Becca didn't strike Lynn as the type who needed to show off to feel better about herself. The woman was the epitome of the four *C*s: cordial, confident, competent and capable.

That left one alternative. Nash had sent her to spy on Lynn.

Becca's mouth hitched into a half grin. "My motto is never stop. Learning. Practicing. Preparing. I come here so I don't get rusty. After every class, I spar one-on-one with either Charlie or Rocco."

"That's smart." Made sense for someone in

her line of work. Lynn's suspicion was in overdrive and misplaced. She needed to decompress. Her vacation with her bestie starting tomorrow couldn't come soon enough.

"I won't be at the next class," Becca said, "but will I see you at my office holiday party with Nash? It's the one time of year we let our hair down with civilians."

"Oh, um…" The question caught her off guard, making Lynn's stomach twist into a pretzel. She thought everyone was well aware of their status. News spread in this small town quicker than pink eye in a preschool. It was hard to keep your personal affairs private. "No. Nash and I broke up."

A poker face replaced Becca's smile, dimming the light in her eyes. "Really? I hadn't heard. Not that Nash is into sharing. But a breakup would explain a lot."

A lot?

Two little words that held so much meaning.

Lynn was tempted to ask, but the answer would only lead to more questions about Nash. The last person she wanted to think about, much less discuss.

"Well," Becca said, "if you change your mind about the extra practice, let me know."

"Will do."

Lynn slipped on her down parka, slung the straps of her purse and gym bag on her shoulder. Forcing herself to push past the soul-deep ache that never left her, she shoved through the front door out onto Third Street. The freezing wind hit her like a hard slap, but she shuffled through it. Her SUV was parked in the lot of the grocery store. It was in the opposite direction of her family's restaurant, Delgado's Bar & Grill, where Nash often had dinner.

Parking two blocks away might seem excessive, but she didn't want to risk running into him. Besides, the extra walk helped her get in her daily steps.

Christmas wreaths and white string lights adorned the lampposts lining the busy street. Every shop window she passed was decorated. Each time a store's front door opened, holiday music flowed from inside.

She used to love this time of year. It had once been her favorite. In fact, she'd met Nash early December last year. This Saturday would've marked their one-year anniversary if they'd still been a couple.

Now, the sparkling decorations, the twinkling lights, the saccharine music, all made her think of Nash.

Which in turn made her think of that awful night.

The two were inexorably linked.

Lynn sidestepped a woman fumbling with her bags, to keep from bumping into her, and when she looked up, she spotted him.

Tall and broad and brooding. Nash Garner.

Her breath froze and then burned in her lungs as her feet faltered to a halt. He strode down the sidewalk, making a beeline in her direction.

His gaze locked with hers, and it all came back to her in a sickening rush.

ANDY CROMBIE.

Locking herself inside Rich's office. Gunfire. Rich being shot. Lynn crouched on the floor behind the desk. Paralyzed in fear. Andy pointed the gun at her head.

The feel of the Ruger in her hand.

The next thing she knew, Nash was rushing around the desk and then kneeling in front of her. He was speaking, but it took a moment for things to come back into focus. For his words to penetrate as he took the gun from her fingers.

She didn't remember pulling the trigger. She didn't hear the last gunshot, but the Ruger had gone off. She'd felt its kick, the sensation almost filtered, as though it were someone else's memory.

But it was hers.

She'd killed Andy Crombie.

THE MEMORY BURNED like acid.

Maybe it wasn't too late to avoid a run-in with him. She spun around and took five steps before the sound of his gruff voice made her hesitate.

"Lynn! Lynn, please wait."

A strong hand clasped her shoulder, turning her around.

It took only an instant for her to absorb every detail about him. Granite features. Hard, square jaw. Collar-length dark hair that was longer than she remembered. Two-day old stubble that formed a barely-there beard and mustache. He wore a black cowboy hat—his usual cutter—a sheep-skin jacket, jeans and boots. His muscular six-four build blocked out the rest of the world, or maybe it was the sheer power of his presence.

She gritted her teeth against the punch of attraction coiling through her.

His face wasn't pretty but definitely striking in a wounded, fallen angel sort of way. Exactly her type. Unfortunately.

His leather-gloved hand left her shoulder and glided down her arm, caressing along the way, conjuring a flutter in her chest—a wave of jumbled emotions so strong and unsettling she wanted to break free and bolt.

But his piercing gray eyes pinned her to the spot.

She should've taken one of his many calls and gotten through this over the phone, where she didn't have to see him and be under the microscope of his laser-like focus. Instead, for the first time in five weeks, they were face-to-face.

Chapter Four

Nash silently thanked Becca for cluing him in that Lynn was taking a class every Thursday evening at USD. He'd played it off as though he'd already been aware. Without that tidbit of essential information, who knows how much longer he would've been forced to go without talking to her, unless he'd resorted to stalking her at home. Something he'd been extremely tempted yet prudently reluctant to do.

A "happenstance" encounter in public was far better.

"Finally." He was thrilled to see her. His spirits instantly lifted and just as quickly dampened. He was burning with too much frustration to muster a smile. "I've been trying to reach you."

Sliding his hand down her arm to cup her elbow, he desperately tried to ignore how his body instantly came alive when touching her.

Lynn stiffened and shrugged free of his grasp. "I got your messages."

He waited for her to continue, to give him a damn explanation for not returning a single phone call. "And?"

"And what?" she asked, looking genuinely confounded.

"I've been worried sick about you."

Biting her bottom lip, she lowered her eyes. "No need to worry. I'm fine."

Now she was lying to his face. Everything about her, from the dark circles under her eyes, the tension in her posture, the noticeable pounds she'd dropped from her already-lean figure, to taking self-defense classes at USD told him she was anything but fine.

"What's going on with you?" he demanded.

She crossed her arms, defiance flashing in her whiskey-brown eyes. "Nothing."

This was so foreign to him. Lynn had always been eager to communicate, the one pressing him to open up and share. Well, the tables had turned, and he didn't like it one little bit.

"I can tell when you're lying," he snapped.

Lynn shook her head, her patience visibly wearing thin. "Go to the grill and have dinner. Don't worry about me. My problems are no longer any of your concern."

The matter-of-fact words were like a knife in his heart.

"I know how precious your time is," she added, without a hint of sarcasm, "and I'm sure you have better things to do." From her tone and expression, she honestly believed that.

They might not be a couple anymore, but if Lynn had a problem, it would always be cause for concern to him. There was nothing he wouldn't do for her.

That would never change.

"I can't bear the thought of you hating me." He had no idea where the admission came from, but he was glad the truth had slipped out, because she softened.

Sadness snuffed out the fire in her eyes. "I don't hate you." Even her voice softened.

As he looked into her beautiful face, all he wanted was to be closer to her, pull her against his chest and wrap his arms around her. But he had to keep his distance or else she might take off like a jackrabbit. "Feels like it. You won't take my calls. You run from me on the street." He swept an errant lock of hair that had gotten loose from her bun back behind her ear.

So much for keeping his distance.

His gaze fell to her lips. Those full lips he could kiss for hours. She was wearing the berry-colored gloss he liked. It tasted as good as it looked.

He tore his focus from her mouth and met her eyes.

"I didn't run, and I don't hate you. Honestly. I never could." Tightening her grip on her gym bag, she shuffled backward until his fingers, which were still caressing her soft skin, fell from her face.

At least she hadn't slapped his hand away, but she was making it clear she'd rather not be touched. Not by him, anyway.

Lynn took another step. "I need to go home and get cleaned up. Have a good—"

"Can I walk you to your car?" he asked, and she looked back at him, as if unsure what to say or do. This was an opportunity to get answers to his questions. He had to seize it. "Where are you parked?"

She frowned. "The grocery store."

Not surprising. Parking at Delgado's would've been closer to USD, but he frequented the bar and grill ever since he'd met her there, and it was painfully obvious Lynn was doing her best to steer clear of him.

If only he knew why.

"You can walk me on one condition," she said.

He drew closer, keen to have more time with her, even if it was mere minutes. She was talking to him, sort of, letting him escort her. Baby steps he'd have to accept. "Name it."

"You don't ask me any more questions."

Nash had a laundry list of those clogging his brain, which she'd rightfully expected and didn't want. If he was going to be in her presence, it had to be on her terms. For now.

He nodded, and his breath crystallized in the air as he said, "Deal."

A snowflake drifted down as they walked, followed by another. He longed to take her hand the way he used to when they'd stroll together, but instead he clenched his gloved fingers. He didn't want to push it and completely blow it tonight.

"I'm worried about you," he said. "I get the sense that you're not coping well with what you've been through. It can be difficult."

She shoved her hands in her pockets. Silence stretched between them until it became awkward. Tense. He was beginning to think that she wasn't going to respond.

Then she looked at him, her eyes haunted. "We all cope, in our own way." A quiet desperation deepened the lines in Lynn's forehead and around her mouth. "I'm doing my best."

He didn't doubt it. "Keeping things bottled up inside isn't healthy."

She gave him a baleful look for throwing her own words back at her. "Thanks for the sage words, Dr. Garner."

"All I'm saying is that you don't have to go through this alone. I'm here for you, to listen, any time." The good doctor obviously needed to start taking her own advice and talk to someone. "Even as just a friend, if that's what you want." *Friend.* He wasn't sure he'd ever really be able to think of her that way, but to help Lynn, he was willing to give anything a try.

Shaking her head, she avoided his gaze. "We can't be friends."

"Wh—" He swallowed the question burning his

tongue, remembering his promise and not wanting to break it.

Time evaporated in the short distance of two blocks. The parking lot was in sight, across the street. It was now or never to clear the air.

"I think about you," he blurted out. "About us. All the time." He'd never felt more vulnerable. Exposed.

He'd been raised to believe there was no need to spill your guts. The proof was in the pudding so to speak, and the pudding was a man's actions. It was better to show those closest to you how much they meant.

Lynn shivered. He hoped from the cold and not from his confession.

"That's why we can't be friends." Emotion he couldn't name flickered across her face, and she glanced away. "Give it a few months. By then, our relationship will be a memory and you'll have moved on to someone new."

He didn't want to move on, to be with someone new, for their relationship to become nothing more than a fading memory.

He wanted Lynn. A few months, heck, a few years, wasn't going to change that.

But her theory registered, sinking beneath the surface like an itch he couldn't scratch.

Had Lynn been avoiding him to give herself time to move on? Had she already found someone new?

She stopped at the corner. "I'm okay here. Good night." She gave him a tense grin before looking both ways and darting across the street.

He couldn't shake the sense that he was going to lose her forever if he didn't say something. Anything.

"Lynn," he called out, "I'm sorry."

She glanced back at him across the street. The wind whipped stray locks of hair in her face. "For what?"

For not wearing his heart on his sleeve the way she had wanted. For not being an open book. For getting caught up at work and being late that night. For not getting to her sooner. For not being the one to shoot Andrew Crombie, so she didn't have to.

"For everything I did wrong."

Flashing him a smile so sad it damn near broke his heart, she held up a hand goodbye.

An apology didn't mean a thing to her. Not that he blamed her.

Nash cursed himself for his endless capacity to destroy any good in his life. All he had left was the FBI. Although he was great at his job, it was sucking his soul dry. At his core he was a lawman, like his father before him and his brothers. He couldn't fathom being anything else.

There was a time when he'd been quicker to smile, to joke around, to share his thoughts. A time when he'd been an easier man to get along with. Eight years in the army and four with the

FBI had worn off any boyhood charm. At thirty-four, he was not a man who engaged in small talk, wasted time on pleasantries or pretended that a situation was anything other than what it was.

Lynn had liked him anyway until she broke things off.

One more thing he'd ruined.

A gust of icy wind sliced through him as he stood there, unable to take his gaze off her. Crossing the well-lit lot over to her SUV, she pressed her key fob, and the lights flashed on her two-door Land Rover Defender.

Lynn threw her purse and gym bag in the passenger's seat, climbed in and closed the door. After cranking the engine, she pulled off and made a right out of the lot. A left turn and taking Third Street would've been the faster route for her to get home, but she probably wanted to avoid passing her pining ex, who was standing on the corner, watching her like a stalker.

Way to go, Nash.

This was shaping up to be a banner evening. Maybe after dinner and a beer with his buddy Holden Powell over at Delgado's and then some solid shut-eye, he'd feel better, though he doubted it.

As he was about to walk away, she passed a lamppost—the light from the streetlamp washing inside the SUV—and he glimpsed a dark blur emerge from the back seat behind Lynn.

Nash's gut clenched as he doubted his eyes. Was someone inside her vehicle?

Chapter Five

I'm sorry.

Two words Nash Garner rarely used. Certainly not lightly. Perhaps that was the reason they carried so much weight with Lynn.

If only what had been the problem between them could be fixed with an apology.

Glancing at the corner of Third Street, Lynn didn't want to pass by Nash, who stood watching her. Or worse, get caught at the traffic light beside him and have to force a smile and give another wave bye. It had been hard enough seeing him, talking to him, being so close she could've reached out and touched him.

When he'd tucked her hair behind her ear, brushing her skin with his fingers, all she wanted was to curl up in his arms, where she'd always felt safe. Her face heated thinking about it. Nash was all male and more enticing than any man she'd ever met. She desperately wanted to lose herself in him. Only guilt had made her pull away. She didn't want to use him for comfort. No matter how much she needed it. She couldn't let herself off the hook, to allow herself to feel better. Especially not with Nash.

Theirs was a complicated relationship with a capital *C*.

A pang of loneliness howled through her like the wind outside.

Instead of going toward Third, she turned right onto Lewis Street, away from Nash. The easier choice albeit not the fastest.

Something hard jabbed into the back of her head.

"Make a left at the corner," a male voice said from behind her.

Lynn's chest convulsed. She looked up into the rearview mirror.

In the back seat was a man. She couldn't see what he was holding in the darkness, but she assumed it was a gun. If it had been a knife, she would've felt the sharpness of the blade.

"I said to turn." The man nudged her head with what she guessed was the muzzle of a pistol.

The command snapped her attention back to the road. Her heart pounded wildly against her sternum as adrenaline flooded her veins, but her thoughts were clear.

Stay calm. Stay alive. Breathe.

Drawing air into her lungs, deep and steady, she forced herself to comply, doing as he instructed. The left turn kept her on a side street with limited traffic, two other cars ahead, no pedestrians. Even if she passed someone on the road, she had no idea what she could do. Signaling a passerby was out of the question so long as he held that gun.

Her mind flooded with terrifying possibilities

of what could happen, but she shoved them all to the side. Imagining the worst wasn't going to help her get out of this. She hadn't survived that horrendous night with Andy to die today.

Not today, she told herself. *Not today.* "What do you want? Where are we going?"

"Keep driving," he said, his mouth close to her ear.

That voice. It was familiar. One she'd heard somewhere before.

Her gaze flashed up to the mirror again for another look at him. A full-face black ski mask covered his head. It was made of a smooth material. A skeleton skull pattern was printed over the face. Only his eyes were visible. Cold. Dark. Steely.

Those she didn't recognize.

"Turn here. Another left."

She rolled through the intersection, ignoring the stop sign, hoping someone might notice as she made the turn.

"Do that again, and I'll hurt you." With his other hand, he reached over the front of her seat and seized her throat in a savage grip, pinning her head back against the seat, and squeezed her windpipe. "Do you understand?"

Panic erupted alongside pain. Lynn gasped, struggling for air. She nodded as best she could. "Yes."

His fingers loosened from around her throat until he released her.

She coughed and sucked in a deep lungful of oxygen. Her hands clutched the steering wheel in a death grip. Her stomach tightened, but she kept herself from succumbing to the fear.

"We can do this the easy way, or the painful way. You decide." His voice was harsh, but his tone was controlled.

This man wasn't unhinged, acting on emotion. He was completely self-possessed. Aware of what he was doing. Calculating his responses.

Somehow that made the situation far more chilling.

As she approached the next intersection, she glanced around, searching for one of the sheriff's telltale white SUVs, a pedestrian whose eye she might catch, anything. But her captor had her sticking to the more isolated pockets of town, away from the two main veins of activity, Third Street and Grand Avenue.

Heading down Russell, she tried to remember if anything would be open down here. What was located on this street?

An elementary school. A taxidermy. What else?

"There." He pointed, reaching over the seat, and she followed the direction of his leather-clad finger to a small building that was dark with no cars in the lot. "The Plainsman Bank. Pull up to the ATM drive-through."

Lynn exhaled, relieved. He wanted money, and once he got it, this could be over. But her relief quickly soured. She was aware how often robberies went wrong. How easily a life could be taken over a couple hundred bucks. A few grams of meth. A pair of sneakers. Or far less. Sometimes there was no explanation at all as to why the victim had been murdered. Just a senseless loss of life. She'd heard countless stories from Nash and the chief deputy, Holden. Not to mention from her own brother, who was also law enforcement back in Denver, Colorado.

After she entered her code in the machine, he could decide to kill her.

Tears pricked the backs of her eyes. If she wasn't careful, she might not leave that drive-through alive.

Come up with a plan.

"Do it, slowly," he said.

She pulled into the lot and maneuvered her Defender between the concrete pillar and the wall as she drew close to the teller machine. Too late, it occurred to her that there had been a chance for her to leave a gap large enough for her to open the door and squeeze through. Now there was no room to get out while they waited for the cash. She'd blocked herself in.

Reaching for her purse to get her debit card, she wondered if she'd be able to find the small canister of pepper spray inside her handbag before he realized what she was doing. Ever since Andy, she stopped carrying the Ruger in favor of a nonlethal deterrent. Maybe, if she was fast enough, she could spray him, press on the gas pedal to clear the pillar and make a break for it. Could she do it all without him getting off a shot first?

"Give it to me." He snatched the purse from her hands, extinguishing what little hope she had for the flimsy idea, and scrounged through her handbag. The weapon lifted from the back of her head, but not long enough for her take any action. Finding the wallet, he tossed her purse up front into the passenger's footwell. "Which card is it?"

"The light blue one. Cowboy State Credit Union." In front of the passenger's seat, her handbag sat open. The pink top of the pepper spray was visible. She'd have to reach pretty far over to grab it from the footwell. Doing so with her seat belt on would be tough and even if she made it, her timing had to be just right.

"Here." He handed her the card while keeping a hold of her wallet.

"How much should I take out?" Her voice wavered and cracked like she was about to cry. Something she refused to do. Not here. Not now.

The cold hardness of steel returned to the back of her head. "Withdraw the max."

Closing her eyes, she swallowed and tried to think, but she didn't have any other choice besides doing what he demanded. All she could do was pray for the best, that he'd take the cash and leave her alone, and not shoot her, dump her body on the side of the street and steal her car.

With trembling fingers, she hit the button on the door, rolling down the window, and inserted her card. Quickly, she punched in the PIN and scanned the words on the screen.

"The ATM limit is three hundred at this machine," she said. That gave her a slim opening, something to work with. She had to give him a reason to keep her alive. "But my daily limit is a thousand." A renewed sense of determination surged in her veins. "I can get you the rest if we go to different machines." Somewhere more populated. There weren't many ATMs like this one, located off the beaten path. She'd forgotten it even existed. "We can go to the one next to the big-box store off Grand." The superstore was open until eleven and thanks to the well-populated area stayed busy until it closed. That was her best chance. "It's not far and the limit at that one is five hundred."

The promise of a thousand dollars in one night had to be a decent score for robbing one person.

She had plenty of money—almost a hundred grand. Granted, it was split between her solo 401(k) and brokerage investment account for a down payment on a house. Not that she had access to either pool of funds at an ATM. Her checking account on the other hand had nowhere near five hundred left in it after this withdrawal since she'd already paid her bills. But this guy didn't know that, and she'd figure a way out of this before the transaction was declined.

"It'll only take a few minutes to get there," she said. Once in the active lot, a whole world of possibilities would open. Honk her horn to attract attention. Dive for the pepper spray. Simply jump from the vehicle and run for it.

"Shut up." He whacked the cold steel against her cheek. Not hard enough to break bone, but plenty to silence her.

Tomorrow she'd have a bruise. If she was lucky enough to live that long.

"When I want your suggestion, I'll ask for it," he growled.

Turning to the machine, she entered in the max amount of three hundred. Seconds ticked by as the machine hummed. She pressed against the seat while rubbing her face and looked back at him. He'd slid over behind the passenger's seat, probably positioning himself to avoid being captured on the ATM's camera. From this angle, he wouldn't be seen, but she now had a clear view of his weapon.

An automatic 9mm. With an attached sound suppressor.

Her blood turned to ice.

Ordinary criminals didn't use silencers, though they were easy enough to come by. Nelson's Gun and Outdoor Sports shop sold them. Could probably get one used that cost even less than the amount she was being forced to withdraw from the ATM over at a pawnshop.

But what kind of lowlife robber used one?

Maybe a smart one. A serious guy who meant business and didn't want to draw unwanted attention when he fired his weapon.

She gulped. Cold sweat beaded along her forehead. Her stomach twisted.

The machine spat out the bills. She took them and handed him the wad of twenties. Out of habit, she reached a shaking hand back to get the receipt.

"Leave it." The command was sharp. "Drive. Now."

Not bothering to roll up the window, she pulled off.

"Hang a right," he said.

Doing as he instructed was taking them in the general direction of the big-box store. Hope spurted inside her. The plan could work. She wouldn't know for certain if that's where they might be headed until this road came to a three-way intersection, when she would be forced to make another turn. She was too afraid to ask him any questions, not wanting to tick this guy off again.

Despite the frosty air flowing in from the open window, sweat trickled down her spine. She clenched the steering wheel, holding her breath as they came to the T-intersection across from the park.

At the stop sign, she cranked the wheel, preparing to go to the left, toward the lights and activity about a half mile away.

"Don't even think about it," he said. "We're heading the other way. Go." He waved the gun at the windshield.

Why didn't he want the rest of the money? She had promised him a thousand dollars.

Her fingers tingled as cold set in. Lynn turned the SUV to the right. Toward the darkness. She caught a glimpse of the street sign, South Corthell Road, and it occurred to her where it led.

Panic tightened in her throat. *No, no, no.*

Traffic didn't come this way. The lights on the utility poles didn't even work on the isolated stretch of road. There would be no stores. No houses. No sidewalks. Not a sole pedestrian. No possibility of help.

There was nothing down that way, besides a barren field and a dead end, and no *good* reason to take her down this dark road.

Her racing heart dropped into the pit of her stomach. She looked up into the rearview mirror. Their gazes met. His unflinching stare was so cruel it sent a chill through her. He held the gun rock-steady in his grip. His body language was rigid in coiled readiness, a cobra measuring its prey.

In the faint gleam of his eyes, his intent was clear. Pure malice.

He was going to rape her. Or kill her.

Or worse, do both.

Her mind went to Nash. Whatever happened, Lynn had to live through this. She couldn't die with him thinking she hated him. So many things she hadn't told him. He deserved an explanation as to why she'd been avoiding him these past weeks. She owed him better than the silent treatment. Nash had endured his fair share of hardship, but having her ripped from his life in a brutal way might break him.

The full moon cast light on the grim, stark landscape surrounding her. It was quiet. No one nearby for miles. She glanced around desperately, trying to think of something to do. The pepper spray sat at the top of her purse but was out of reach. Attempting to negotiate, to talk her way out of this, would be a waste of her energy.

With each utility pole she passed, Lynn's dread swelled. Farther and farther, they went into the darkness. Closer and closer to her last breath.

The next time he told her to pull over and stop the vehicle that would be it. The end of her.

Headlights glimmered in the rearview mirror. In the distance. Not too far behind. Another vehicle had turned down the same road and was headed their way.

One more spark of fight burned through her.

Maybe it was just adrenaline. Either way, she wasn't giving in.

Not today. Not ever.

She eased off the gas, slowing down to let the other car catch up to them.

This was her last chance. She sensed it. Time was running out for her. She had to act before he noticed the car that was quickly closing the distance and panicked, doing something rash, like shooting her and taking off.

What would Charlie do?

Her experienced instructor would be able to get out of this situation in a cinch with her martial arts skills. But what would she tell Lynn, a terrified novice, to do right now?

All her training at USD came back to her. Not the fight moves and evasive maneuvers. She heard Charlie's voice in her head, reminding her of the different ways to survive. How to use everything around her to her advantage.

Always Think Outside the Box.

Sucking in a deep, steadying breath, she tightened her grip on the steering wheel. The man in the back seat had a gun trained on her, but she wasn't helpless, and she wasn't unarmed.

She was in the driver's seat of a one-and-a-half-ton weapon. In full control of it.

People were injured and killed in car crashes every day.

And she was the only one wearing a seat belt.

The rear seat could be as deadly as the front when someone was unbuckled.

Her pulse thundered in her ears, but she was focused on what she needed to do.

Headlights from the other car blazed up behind them.

Twisting around, the man looked back through the rear windshield, moving the gun away from her head. "Speed up." He swore, banging the gun on the back seat. "Go faster!"

Her thoughts precisely. Lynn pressed her foot down on the gas pedal. She jerked the wheel to the right. As soon as the tires skidded off the asphalt and hit dirt, she straightened, lining her vehicle up with the utility pole looming dead ahead of them.

"What are you doing?" He grabbed her shoulder and squeezed.

Nausea gripped her. A scream welled up inside her, scraping her throat raw. At almost the last second, fear made her lift her foot off the gas, not wanting to kill anyone else, especially herself, but she didn't dare hit the brakes.

"Stop, damn you!"

Go to hell. Throwing her arms up in front of her face, Lynn looked away as they slammed into the pole.

Chapter Six

Lynn!

With his heart in his throat, Nash zoomed up behind her SUV. Dust whipped around his truck when he screeched to a halt.

In the distance were sirens. Holden would be the first one on the scene. As soon as Nash had suspected Lynn was in danger, he called his buddy. Then he had sprinted to his truck and searched for her vehicle. Found her on Russell Street and observed from a position close to the bank parking lot. He had to be sure that fatigue hadn't been making him see things. Once he'd verified the guy in the back of her car was real and had spotted the gun the man had on her while she withdrew money from the ATM, proceeding with caution became a necessity. As did vigilance. There was no way he was going to take his eyes off her vehicle.

He threw the gear into Park, leaped from his truck and drew his weapon. Worry gripped his chest as he raced up to her SUV. The front end was totaled, twisted around the utility pole. The damage was serious. He yanked open her door and stared down at her.

His terror washed into relief.

The driver's-side airbag had deployed and was

already deflating. She was alive, *thank goodness*; conscious, but a little woozy. His gaze snapped to the rear seat as he trained his weapon in the same direction.

Empty. The passenger's seat had been shoved forward and the back door was flung open. Her assailant was gone.

But he was out there. Somewhere in the darkness. Hiding. Possibly running. Not that Nash could tell either way with the sound of the sirens drawing closer, masking any noise in the vicinity.

He holstered his weapon and unbuckled Lynn's seat belt.

"Nash?" Her wide, frantic eyes locked onto his. "What are you doing here?"

Watching out for you. Something he'd do for as long as he was able. He didn't know how to stop. It was the way he was wired.

"What the hell happened?" He cupped her cheeks in his hands and looked her over. No scrapes on her face. No bloody nose. She was fortunate.

"Wait." She twisted in her seat as if remembering something, her gaze flying to the back. "Where is he?"

"Gone. He took off. The back seat was empty by the time I got to your car." It hadn't taken Nash long. His guess was her assailant wasn't badly injured if he'd been able to get out of the car so quickly and disappear. That didn't mean he was unscathed from the crash. Nash hoped like hell he was in pain. "Did he hurt you?"

She shook her head *no*, but the expression on her face said otherwise.

Flashing lights zipped down the street, illuminating the dark road. A white deputy's vehicle led the way, followed by an ambulance.

Good thinking, Holden.

"What about in the crash?" Nash asked. "Any injuries? Did you hit your head?"

"I don't think so."

It was still possible she might have whiplash or a concussion. "Can you move?"

Nodding, she said, "Yeah."

He helped her climb out of the SUV as the first-responder vehicles pulled up to a stop. She took a couple of steps, and her legs gave way.

Nash scooped her up before she fell. She was shaking uncontrollably in his arms.

"I'm a little dizzy and nauseous, but I can walk," she said, her voice low yet her tone insistent. "You don't have to carry me."

His only response was a grunt. Fighting with her wasn't going to help, so the fewer words he used the better.

"I don't want you to hurt your back," she added, softly.

Unbelievable. She was the one who'd crashed her vehicle after being robbed at gunpoint. Now she was more concerned about him than herself.

But that was the kind of woman Lynn was. Considerate. Caring. Always putting others first.

"You're light," he said. "I'm fine."

Sometimes his back ached. Old injuries from the military flaring up, reminding him they existed. All rangers had to be airborne qualified. Aches, occasional inflammation, sometimes arthritis were typical consequences after being required to jump out of airplanes on a regular basis. But not a stitch of pain bothered him at the moment.

All he felt was adrenaline and worry for Lynn.

Nash made his way to the back of the ambulance where the EMTs had already opened the rear doors. He sat her down inside. "She was in a head-on collision in the driver's seat. Airbag deployed."

The EMTs put her on a gurney and began checking her out.

Holden hopped out of his vehicle, slammed the door and hurried over. "What happened to her vehicle?"

Nash stepped out of Lynn's earshot but stayed where he could keep an eye on her. "She crashed it. On purpose."

"What in the hell?" Holden looked as baffled as Nash felt.

One paramedic took Lynn's blood pressure while the other flashed a light in her eyes and had Lynn track her finger.

"I haven't had a chance to ask her why," Nash

said. But Lynn never acted without a good reason. Same applied to her breaking up with him. She analyzed all the factors, weighed her choices and decided accordingly. "Must've had something to do with the armed guy in her car."

"Is he dead?"

If only they could be so lucky to have this resolved with a corpse in the back seat. "No. He got away. Took off out that way somewhere."

"Did you get a look at him?"

"He was gone by the time I got to her."

Holden keyed his radio. "Dispatch, this is Chief Deputy Powell. Where's my helicopter? Is Mitch in the air yet?"

Mitch Cody was a maverick the new sheriff, Daniel, recruited after procuring additional funding for a law enforcement helicopter. Mitch used to fly Black Hawks for the army. Nash liked him. Sometimes he'd join him and Holden for dinner at Delgado's.

"He's in the air," dispatch responded. "As soon as I notified him of your call, he hustled over as quickly as he could."

Good man. Not a slacker.

"I need him over the barren field off South Corthell Road," Holden said. "We're searching for a fleeing suspect, male, on foot. Dark clothing. That's all I've got for now."

"Roger that," said the dispatcher.

The radio went silent.

"We might spot him," Holden said to Nash. "It's worked before, and Mitch is pretty fast."

Nonetheless, Mitch's response time wouldn't be fast enough. Nash sensed it in his gut, despite his desire for this to go in their favor. Spot the guy, vector to his position and arrest him—end of story.

"Two close calls for Lynn in less than two months." Holden clasped Nash's shoulder. "My mom would say these things come in threes."

Nash clenched his jaw. Ever since that night at Turning Point, it had been lurking at the edge of his mind, the dark possibility of *the next time*. He was grateful she wasn't dead behind the wheel of her car or lying on this dark road in the freezing cold with a team of crime-scene techs surrounding her.

"Let's hope Mrs. Powell is wrong." Nash didn't know how much more Lynn could handle.

She was a strong woman, but this wasn't a matter of strength. Everyone had their breaking point. All he knew was he couldn't take it if anything happened to her.

That was the secret fear of everyone in law enforcement. Being unable to prevent something horrible from happening to their loved ones.

"All right, go be with Lynn." Holden pulled out a pair of latex gloves and tugged them on. "I'll take a look around her car. Once the paramedics clear her, I can ask her a few questions."

"Okay."

Unhooking a flashlight from his utility belt, his friend trekked toward the crash site, and he went to check on Lynn.

HOLDEN POWELL EXAMINED the driver's-side door first. Taking a good look at the window and door handle, he found several small scratches near the lock and along the base of the window frame. That's where the guy had gotten in.

But her car alarm should've gone off. It would've drawn a lot of attention. Once that happened, most perps grabbed whatever they could, any high-value items in the car, and bolted.

Flashing his light inside, he crouched down and peeked in, up under the dash. Powder from the deflated airbag lingered in the air, itching his throat. He spotted what he was looking for. Wires for the alarm had been pulled, sliced and tucked out of the way so Lynn wouldn't notice when she first got into her vehicle.

This wasn't an impromptu job of someone like a junkie, desperate for some quick cash to get their next fix. Whoever did this had taken the time to prepare and plan and had the patience to wait for Lynn.

A good thing Nash had spotted the man in her back seat, or this night could've ended much differently.

He pushed her seat forward and flashed the

light around the back. Maybe the robber had dropped something, slipped up and left behind a clue that might help identify him.

Nothing on the rear seat or the floor. The inside was tidy. He checked the seam at the very back of the seat to be sure. No loose change, no papers, no keys. There wasn't even a gum wrapper.

Holden climbed out and went around to the front of the vehicle and inspected the damage from the collision. The impact had crushed the front. From the looks of it, he guessed it was mainly the frame and that the engine was probably intact. Still, her vehicle was an older model. The insurance company would consider it a complete loss and cut her a check rather than pay to have it repaired. Good insurance would even pay for a rental.

The sound of the helicopter he noticed first, followed by the bright spotlight washing over the adjacent barren field. It had taken a little longer than he would've preferred for Mitch to get out there, but considering the guy hadn't been on duty, his response time was impressive. The circumstances that brought Daniel Clark to the Albany County Sheriff's Department weren't pleasant, and Holden would rather not think on it at all, but Daniel had been a good fit for the department, even managing to get them their first law enforcement helicopter.

Moving to the other side of the Defender, he

swept the beam of his flashlight over the passenger's door. His suspicion was confirmed that the suspect had gotten in on the driver's side when there weren't marks or scratches on this door.

A dark spot on the frame caught his attention. Under the light, he made it out. Blood. The man's hand had touched blood and it was smeared on the side frame as he pressed his palm there for leverage when getting out of the car.

It was the same on the back of the seat that had been shoved forward as well as the inner door handle.

No other apparent traces had been left behind, but this was the next best thing to the guy dropping his ID.

In the front, he spotted Lynn's purse and larger bag. He shone his light on both as he went through the contents. Next, he checked her glove box and the inside of her center console.

A couple of things worried him. Hopefully, Lynn would erase at least one of those concerns when she answered his questions.

After he contacted dispatch to have a crime-scene tech come out, he grabbed both bags and did a cursory once-over of the rear of the car.

An etching on the bumper, where the paint had been scraped off, glinted in the light. He got down low, balancing on the balls of his feet, for a closer look.

He cursed under his breath.

It can't be.

Holden wanted to be mistaken about the engraving that had been keyed into her car, but the longer he stared at it the more certain he was of what it meant.

Lynn was in grave danger.

Chapter Seven

The wind gusted, sending a spray of ice crystals over Nash. He shivered from the cold, his back now starting to ache. The brisk chill made him feel all his thirty-four years on the planet and then some. Standing at the rear of the ambulance in between the open doors, he shielded himself as best he could from the cold. His black Stetson was clamped on tight against the wind. He stayed out of the way of the EMTs and listened as they finished examining her.

"How fast were you going when you hit the pole?" the slim, lanky paramedic asked.

"I can't be sure." Lynn laced her fingers together and squeezed, like she was trying to stop them from shaking. "But I eased off the gas at the last minute. I think the speedometer dropped somewhere below fifty."

"It's a good thing you slowed down," he said, charting the patient care report on a tablet. "If you hadn't, you might be in worse condition."

From the looks of her vehicle, if she had been going any faster when she'd hit the utility pole, the impact harder, she might not have survived. "So, how is she?" Nash asked.

"No concussion," the other paramedic said, kneeling beside the gurney. She was a petite blonde, with her hair in a braid down her back. "No internal injuries. Whiplash is still a possibility. Symptoms don't always present immediately."

Lynn leaned forward, holding on to her knees, and winced. "Ouch." She held up her left arm, taking the pressure off it.

"Let's have a look." Her coat was already off, and the tech pulled up the sleeve of her sweatshirt gingerly. There was a cut on her forearm, the skin split, angry red and bleeding. "Did you hit your arm against anything in the crash?"

Lynn thought for a moment. "Only the airbag. I threw my arms up in front of my face, instinctively, right before the collision."

The two EMTs exchanged a look. Then the one standing said, "That explains why you don't have a single mark on your face. Those airbags can do a number on a person."

Nash knew firsthand how true that was. He'd once been in a car chase with a suspect that had ended with the perpetrator crashing. The force exerted on a person's face when there was a collision caused you to smash into the airbag. It could easily fracture your nose, dislocate your jaw, damage the eyes. The perp hadn't walked away from the accident.

"Will she need stitches?" Nash wondered.

"No. The cut isn't deep. I can take care of it." The paramedic cleaned the wound and applied a series of butterfly bandages to the slash on her arm. "Tomorrow don't be alarmed in the event you have any pain or soreness in other places. It's common, but if you experience anything severe, you should see a doctor. Tonight, be sure to ice the arm."

"I will, along with my cheek." She pressed a palm to the right side of her face.

Nash stepped closer, noticing the pink mark on her skin. A bruise was forming. "I thought you said you didn't hit your head?"

"I didn't. The guy smacked my cheek with his gun."

He inwardly winced, though anger burned through him. If he ever got his hands on that man, Nash would make him regret the night he climbed into Lynn's car.

She must have read the intent on his face. "I'll be fine, really. Whatever you're thinking, Nash, you can forget about it."

He tilted his head up to the night sky and sighed. All he was doing was reaffirming the reasons why Lynn thought they wouldn't work as a couple and had ended things between them. His propensity for violence. His use of compartmentalization, which made him emotionally unavailable. The fact that he was a workaholic control freak.

She had even said that they didn't speak the same love language. Whatever that meant.

There was uncomfortable truth to the things

she'd brought up months ago. So much so that he had been unable to deny any of it, but that wasn't his whole story.

"Well, ice both and take an NSAID," said the paramedic. "You should feel better in the morning."

"I hope so." Lynn put on her coat. "I'm going on vacation tomorrow."

Nash thrust his hands into the pockets of his parka. That was news to him. He had no idea what was going on with her since she shut him out. He also had no right to ask the question at the forefront of his mind. Instead, he decided to bide his time and bit his tongue.

The EMT lowered the tablet. "Where are you going?"

"Mountain cabin retreat."

Maybe there was a new guy in her life after all. Lynn wasn't the type to go away alone.

"You deserve a vacation after this. Somewhere special," one of the EMTs said.

"It's nothing fancy." Lynn clutched her hands as a small smile graced her lips. "We're staying in state. But I think it'll be special."

He caught the "we're." She definitely wasn't going alone.

An unwanted surge of jealousy sent a sharp pain through him. The only thing worse than that awful feeling was the fear that had gripped him when Lynn's car crashed. He wanted her to be healthy, happy and safe, even if it wasn't with him.

"Hope you two enjoy the trip." The paramedics looked at Nash.

"Oh, I'm not going with him," Lynn said, dropping her gaze and drawing everyone's attention once again. "I'm, uh, going with my best friend."

Yvonne Lamber. She moved to Cheyenne this past summer after she got a big promotion to executive manager for a local hotel chain. The two women had gotten close quickly when Lynn relocated to Laramie to help out her aunt. Miriam Delgado had Alzheimer's and could no longer handle things at the bar and grill. The first to pitch in whenever family needed assistance, Lynn uprooted herself from Colorado, put her real job on hold and worked sixteen-hour days managing the restaurant until she found a stable replacement. Eventually she got her aunt settled in the Silver Springs senior living center, where Lynn visited her as much as possible.

Laramie was a close-knit community full of good people willing to lend a hand. Everyone did what they could to help. Even if it was something as small as patronizing the living heck out of Delgado's the way he and Holden did.

That's how he had met Lynn. Over the Wednesday special plate of meat loaf with garlic mashed potatoes and green beans.

Lynn was tireless, working nonstop. Caring for

her aunt. Volunteering at the community center. Keeping an eye on Delgado's, filling in when they were short on staff. As well as treating clients.

A vacation would do her good, especially after tonight. If anybody deserved one, it was her. He regretted that they'd never been able to take one together. They'd both been too busy.

Holden approached them. "Are you going to be okay, Lynn?"

She nodded and slid down to the end of the gurney. "Besides a cut on my arm and a sore cheek, I was given a clean bill of health."

The EMTs moved toward the front of the ambulance and started putting away supplies and equipment.

"That's good to hear." Holden gave a tight smile. "I'm happy to say the perpetrator didn't get away uninjured."

"What do you mean?" Nash asked.

"I found a bloody handprint on the seat that he shoved forward to get out, on the inside door handle, and side of the car. My guess is that he hit his face, probably got a bloody nose and wiped it with his hand."

"You won't be able to pull any fingerprints," Lynn said. "He was wearing gloves."

"But now we've got his DNA. If we're lucky, we'll get a hit on a match in the system," Holden said, meaning the FBI's CODIS—Combined

DNA Index System—which was used by law enforcement labs nationwide.

The database linked unknown DNA left during the commission of a crime to offenders who were legally required to provide samples. The hitch was they'd only learn his identity if the guy was a previously convicted criminal or had a DNA swab upon arrest in one of the states that allowed taking it without a conviction.

"A crime-scene tech is on the way. In the meantime, Lynn, can you run me through precisely what happened?" Holden asked.

"Sure. I left USD, like I do every Thursday. Ran into Nash. He walked me to where my car was parked."

"Actually, she stopped me at the corner of Third and Lewis," Nash said. "I watched her walk the rest of the way to the grocery store lot by herself." If he had been less pushy, she might've let him walk her up to her vehicle and this whole mess might've been avoided.

"When I got in my car, I was wrapped up in my own thoughts, distracted." She glanced at Nash. "I didn't realize the man was in my back seat until I had turned out of the lot."

Not only had he been too aggressive in his approach with her, but he'd also been the source of her distraction. "That's when I thought I saw someone and called you."

Holden nodded slowly, taking in the details. "Did you get a look at him?"

"No." Lynn shook her head. "He wore a black ski mask with a skull face painted on it. All I could see were his eyes, but it was too dark to make out the color."

"Go on," Holden said.

"He forced me to drive to the bank at gunpoint and withdraw the max."

"How did you end up on this road with your car wrapped around that pole?" Holden hiked a thumb back at the crashed vehicle.

"He made me turn this way at the intersection," Lynn said. "I had offered to go to another ATM to get him more money, but he didn't go for it. That's when he hit me and told me to shut up. When he demanded that I drive down here, where there were no lights, complete isolation, I realized he intended to kill me. I saw Nash's headlights behind us, but I didn't know it was him. That's when I had the *brilliant* idea to crash my SUV." Sarcasm dripped from her voice. "I figured it would stop the guy in the back seat. At the very least, slow him down long enough for the other driver to intervene."

Quick thinking for certain, albeit reckless.

"Was there anything distinctive about him?" Holden asked. "Did he speak with an accent, a lisp, a stutter?"

"No, nothing I can think of."

"What about his build?"

"I'd say about your height." Lynn gestured to Holden. "Around six feet. Not as lean as you. Slightly more muscular, like Nash, but not as wide-shouldered."

"Did he mention or say anything that stood out? Give any indication why he targeted you?"

"Not that I can recall."

"Did he say outright that he was going to kill you?" Holden asked.

Squeezing her eyes shut a moment, she shook her head. "No, but I could tell. I felt it. His intention to do me harm."

Maybe it had been the nature of the situation, like when you're walking down a dark street and you feel someone getting too close. Maybe it had been that Lynn was sensitive and good at reading people. Either way, Nash believed her when she said that man had intended to kill her.

"Okay. That gives us something to go on." Holden handed Lynn her purse and gym bag. "I do have a couple of immediate concerns. The first being that your gun wasn't in your purse or anywhere in your car."

Nash had shared with Holden when he'd given Lynn the handgun as a gift and had advised her to keep it on her person. After the incident at Turning Point, everyone in the sheriff's department was aware that Lynn was packing.

"Is it possible the suspect stole it?" Holden continued.

Lynn hesitated. "No." She clenched her hands around her bags. "I don't carry it anymore."

"Why not?" Nash asked, the question coming out harsher than he'd intended. "I told you to carry it with you at all times." He'd insisted until she had agreed. Having that gun on her saved her life that night when he'd been too late and too slow to do it.

Lynn straightened and fixed him with a direct gaze. "Because I got rid of it."

"You did what?" he snapped. "Why?"

"I have my reasons," she said.

"It's always better to be the person holding the gun than the one running from the gunman," Nash said. *Or rather the one crashing into a pole.*

"Amen to that," Holden mumbled under his breath while scrubbing a hand over his jaw.

"Of course you would agree with him." Lynn threw a hand up in resignation.

"What's that supposed to mean?" Holden asked, looking between them.

"Let's just say you two share a similar philosophy about life," she said, making it sound like that was a bad thing. She lifted her chin and stared at Nash. "Can we discuss this at a more appropriate time so your buddy can get on with his job?"

As much as he hated to admit it, she was right. This was not the time or the place for this discussion. "What was your second concern, Holden?"

"Lynn's wallet is missing from her handbag."

Damn it. Credit and debit cards could be frozen with a simple phone call, but that man now had her driver's license, which meant he had her home address.

The impact of the news was visible on Lynn in the shrinking of her shoulders and the slight hunching of her posture, as if she'd taken a blow. "He took it from my purse and handed me my debit card but held on to the wallet." She quickly straightened, recovering, and inhaled a deep though shaky breath. "I forgot that he'd kept it."

"There's one more thing." Holden's tone implied he was reluctant to mention it. "I found a symbol scratched onto your rear bumper." His gaze flew to Nash. "The symbol for a female. A circle with a cross at the bottom."

"That's no big deal, right?" Lynn said. "Some kid must've keyed my car."

But if this was going in the direction that Nash was dreading, then the significance was major.

"It also had a box drawn around it," Holden said to Nash, "with an *X* marked through it."

A sinking sensation dropped in the pit of his stomach. Things just went from bad to a whole helluva lot worse. It also confirmed why that man had brought her down this particular road.

"What does it mean?" Lynn asked.

"Nash, I figured you might want to be the one to tell her."

Lynn scooted to the edge of the gurney. "To tell me what?"

Nash didn't want to alarm her, driving her stress levels any higher, but this situation might not be over. She needed to know. "We've received updates from the Colorado field offices about three cases spanning from Denver to Fort Collins. Women who were stalked and murdered. Each had the symbol Holden described drawn on their rear bumpers. We believe it's the killer's calling card." Nash's office brought the information to the attention of the local police and sheriff's department once a pattern emerged, and it appeared as though the killer might be preparing to cross the border into Wyoming.

"A serial killer?" Another blow. This time blanching the color from her face.

Nash scanned the area. Killers preferred remote locations such as this. It gave them the privacy and time they needed to torture and murder their victims.

Anger slithered through him, but he was careful not to show it.

Holden folded his arms. "Since this guy knows where you live, I have to strongly advise you not to go home tonight. In fact, it's best if you don't go home for a few days," Holden said. "Give us a chance to apprehend him."

Lynn lowered her head and exhaled a harsh breath. "I was planning to spend a long weekend up in the mountains with Yvonne, but we aren't meeting up there until tomorrow afternoon and I haven't even packed. I have to go home to get some things."

"Not alone," Holden said. "And you can't spend the night there."

If this was the same serial killer, then he'd been watching Lynn for a while and knew where she lived long before he'd stolen her wallet. Although she lived across the street from the University of Wyoming Police Department, it gave her a false sense of security. She never even had an alarm system installed. It would be easy enough for someone to break in on the back side of her house, which was shrouded in darkness and tall bushes.

The last place she could stay was at her home.

"I'll take you to your house," Nash offered, "so you can get what you need. You're welcome to stay the night with me. In my guest room," he quickly added. "If that doesn't suit you, I'll drive you to Yvonne's in Cheyenne." It was an hour drive one way. He'd rather not spend two on the road when he was bone-tired and starving, but he'd learned his lesson about being pushy.

Weighing her options, Lynn frowned. "I don't want to inconvenience you, put you through any extra trouble, considering everything you've already done for me. Once I grab my things, you can drop me off at a hotel. I need to go to Turning Point in the morning, and I can make arrangements to have Yvonne pick me up there in the afternoon."

Nash cut his gaze to Holden, who met his exasperated glance. This decision was up to Lynn, but he expected her to make the right one.

"That's not a good idea," Holden said, without Nash needing to utter a word. "You shouldn't be alone tonight. Not just from an emotional perspective, but what if you suddenly get dizzy or a headache or something? It's better to have someone look after you tonight."

Holden had practically read his mind. This was why they were tight. They were cut from the same cloth. Understood each other. Shared a *similar philosophy about life* for sure.

"I can see I'm not going to win this fight," Lynn said. "I know what it takes to challenge one of you, let alone both, and I'm not up for it right now. So I concede. We'll do it your way, Nash. But I have one request."

"Whatever you need."

"Let's not discuss anything else tonight." Weariness clouded her face. "I don't have the energy."

She needed to rest, and he'd see to it that she did. Safely, without interruption.

"You'll have peace and quiet tonight," he promised. "But tomorrow, we'll talk?" His question surprised Holden, who arched his eyebrows in response.

Nash was normally a reticent man. Listening,

observing, digging around, made him good at his job. Not chitchatting. He most certainly didn't request to have conversations.

Things had to be different with Lynn, as she had already made abundantly clear. He was prepared to try to give her what she wanted. One day, one discussion at a time.

First, she had to give him a chance.

"Yes," she said. "Tomorrow, we'll talk. A proper discussion is long overdue."

Good. He couldn't agree more.

They'd wasted too many weeks as it was, and if the man who'd set his sights on Lynn was indeed the serial killer the FBI was hunting in Colorado, better known as TRK, an abbreviated form of *torture, rape, kill*, then he wasn't going to squander any more time. TRK had murdered three women, moving progressively north. Nash wasn't going to let Lynn become the fourth victim.

Chapter Eight

For the past twelve hours, Nash had been the epitome of patience. Considerate beyond belief. Lynn was grateful to him for it. Truth be told, she had needed the quiet, safe space he'd provided. No prodding her to eat dinner when she wasn't hungry last night. No crowding her space. He'd given her a couple of ice packs, some medicine for the pain, ensured she was tucked into his guest room with plenty of water and had bid her good-night.

It was strange, being at his place and not in his bed with him wrapped around her. She missed the feel of him, the smell of him. She missed the comfort mingled with pleasure that he brought. Not that she deserved either from him.

It had taken a while, but once the adrenaline had faded, she'd gotten her first peaceful night's rest in weeks without any nightmares and had even slept in.

Nash had called into work, letting his office know he'd be in late. Made her a home-cooked breakfast of scrambled eggs, bacon and toast. Rather than bombarding her with questions and criticisms while she ate, he'd been silent, pensive. Watching her with those eyes that seemed to see straight into her soul.

Sitting in the passenger's seat of his truck,

she rubbed her arm. More than the laceration on her forearm hurt. Her whole body was sore, but spending time with Nash made her heart ache.

As he pulled into the parking lot across the street from the Turning Point clinic, she realized she couldn't put off the discussion any longer. She feared the prospect of saying something that might hurt him, especially since she was still processing her own emotions over the shooting. She had even begun to tackle how she felt about what happened last night. More so, she dreaded stepping inside the clinic. Every time she crossed the threshold, the building came alive with horrible memories.

Sometimes it took a couple of hours for her anxiety to subside, sometimes most of the day, but it never went away completely.

It hadn't been so long ago when she'd been thankful to work at Turning Point. Once Rich had learned about her aunt, Miriam, a pillar in the community suffering from a neurological disorder, he had graciously offered to let Lynn join his practice. Even helped her build a list of clients. If only she had known where it would lead.

Working at Delgado's and waiting for a position to open at the hospital would have been better.

She peered out the window. From this part of town, there was a view of both the Laramie Mountains and the Snowy Range.

Today was overcast, a leaden sky hanging over Laramie. The temperature was freezing, and the forecast called for heavy snow. Flurries had already started and were sticking to the ground. She couldn't wait to get up to the cabin with Yvonne before the roads got bad and simply relax. Forget about the lethal criminal, a possible serial killer, who had her wallet and knew where she lived. She'd canceled her cards, and would have to rely on Yvonne for money until they were all sorted.

A massive shiver moved through her. She felt sick again, thinking about last night.

As she often told her clients, avoidance didn't solve problems. It often only made a situation worse.

Lynn turned to Nash.

His face was stoic, with no hint as to what he was thinking. His gaze was diffuse, eyes scanning the street all around them, like he was looking for something. Large hands weren't clenched at his sides but were still primed to curl into fists in the blink of an eye if he needed to leap into action. It was as if he was always ready to tackle a threat. His muscled body was still as stone.

"I can understand you wanting to talk to me here," Nash said, indicating the clinic with a nod of his head. "On your turf. Instead of at my place. Whatever is more comfortable for you."

Actually, she had planned to hash over things in *his* truck. She didn't need any perceived position of power. It was sweet of him to worry about her and give up the seeming advantage.

"Before we go inside," he said, "I need you to know something." The intensity of the look he gave her, dark and mysterious as a forest and yet as sharp and cutting as a blade of saw grass, sent a flutter through her chest. "No matter how our conversation ends, I want you to remain in my life. Even if that means only as friends." He offered his hand.

"Nash." She said his name like a curse, her voice thick with emotion.

"No more avoiding me. We started as friends. We can be that again. If it comes to that. Promise me."

She glanced down at his extended hand. The last thing she wanted to do was touch him. Once she got started it would be hard to stop. But if she rebuked this small gesture, then he'd certainly believe she hated him.

"Okay." She put her palm in his.

Brow creased, he looked down at their joined hands. He rubbed the inside of her wrist with his thumb in light, tender circles, the way she used to love.

Those flutters slid from her chest down to her belly.

Damn him.

It was hard to resist a man like Nash. The one area of their relationship where they'd never had a problem and had been a perfect match was in the bedroom. When they had first taken things to an intimate level, they'd spent two straight days between the sheets. Over time, any issue that popped up between them, instead of talking, he sought to resolve by making love to her—sometimes slow, sometimes desperate, always leaving her moved, spent, shaken. She'd succumbed to his seduction so many times, so easily, so eagerly, it had become an unhealthy habit.

Still rubbing those soft circles on the inside of her wrist, he cupped her face with his other hand, sending a rush of uncertainty through her. His touch was warm, careful not to aggravate the bruise on her cheek. "Thank you." His voice was astonishingly gentle.

Gentleness was not something Nash often showed. But it was there, in the touch of his hand on her cheek, in the softness of his voice.

Their gazes locked, and a spark of heat flashed between them hot enough to start a wildfire. Every time she got close to him, there was an underlying current of sexual awareness.

If she didn't get out of this truck and away from him, he'd have her thighs quivering next.

"Nash," she said, this time in a half whisper, not certain if she was asking him to stop or continue.

His gray eyes were stripped of all their usual cool hardness. They were as clear as glass and full of desire. And more. A tenderness she had never seen in them before.

As he leaned in, she realized she was in trouble. Because she wasn't pulling away.

The front door of Turning Point flew open, drawing their attention. Rich staggered outside, fumbling to hold on to a box with a sling around his bad arm that looked like a broken wing.

Nash swore under his breath. He dropped his hands, turned off the engine and hopped out of the truck.

Lynn sighed with relief. Her body was attuned to Nash's, responding with the slightest contact, pushing her to draw closer. At the same time, her head was a conflicting jumble that screamed for her to keep her distance.

Given a few more minutes, seconds if she were being honest with herself, and they would've kissed.

So much for being friends.

She watched Nash hustle across the street to provide assistance.

Saved by Richard Jennings.

TALK ABOUT BAD TIMING. This couldn't have been any worse. Why couldn't Rich have waited two minutes before shoving through the front door?

All Nash had really needed was one, and Lynn would've been in his arms with her lips pressed to his. That would've been a much better way to start their discussion. He always lacked the right words but had no difficulty showing her how he felt about her.

He jogged over and scooped up the cardboard box as it was about to tumble out of the doctor's grasp. A frame tipped over the side, but Nash managed to grab it in midair before it smashed to the ground.

"Thank you," Rich said, looking flustered as he took the frame from Nash's hand. "I'm glad it didn't break. Custom frame. That's my son."

Nash looked down at a magazine cover. It featured a man in his thirties wearing a suit with his arms crossed. The subheading read "Five Minutes with Devin Jennings: Mitigating Artificial Intelligence Concerns."

"He's the cofounder and vice president of Trident Security." Rich beamed as he spoke. "The company has become a real powerhouse. They're based in California. Los Angeles."

"You must be proud."

"I am. Wish his mother had lived to see it. He favors her. Fortunate for him." Rich laughed, moving his bad arm. Wincing, he hissed with pain.

The bullet had struck the bone, fracturing it and complicating his recovery. If it had passed straight through, not hitting anything important, he would've been out of the sling weeks ago.

"Let me help you with this," Nash offered, and they started across the street, where Lynn was waiting next to Rich's car. As they walked, he scanned the contents of the box. It was filled with personal items. A coffee mug, two plants—succulents—a framed PhD, some files, books and a bottle of scotch. "What's all this? Are you leaving the clinic?"

Rich stepped onto the sidewalk near Lynn. "Yes." He glanced at her with a sad smile. "It's time."

Lynn nodded with a sympathetic expression.

"I thought you'd be there providing counseling for another ten years," Nash said. Perhaps longer.

"So did I, but that night…the shooting." Rich adjusted his arm in the sling and winced. "It changed everything for me."

"For both of us," Lynn said, her light brown eyes somber beneath their long black lashes.

"I'm afraid I can't do this anymore," Rich said, "no matter how much a part of me would like to. This is for the best."

"What are you going to do with yourself?" Nash wondered. Rich was middle-aged, but still full of life.

"My son wants me to move out to LA, to be close to him and his kids. I've put my house up for sale. Once it's sold, I'm going to try retirement on the West Coast. Devin is going to buy me a condo with a great view. Walking distance to his place. There'll be plenty to keep me busy, with three grandkids all under the age of five." Rich unlocked his trunk and opened it.

"Sounds like you'll have your hands full." Nash

set the box down in the car and closed the trunk. "When is the retirement party?"

"I don't want to make a fuss."

Rich was the first to throw a party for any reason and invite half the town. There were probably a lot of folks who would've liked the opportunity to say goodbye to him, but then he'd have to rehash the trauma, explaining why he was retiring early.

Nash didn't blame him for not wanting to go through that repeatedly during a party that was supposed to be fun. The man had almost lost his life. His recovery was long and painful. Based on the way Lynn was handling the situation, he imagined Rich was healing not only physically, but mentally, too.

"I thought you'd be here at nine," Rich said to Lynn. "When you didn't show, I packed up my stuff and left my keys in the top drawer of my desk."

"I'm sorry I'm late." Lynn tensed. "I had an incident last night. I was mugged and my car was totaled. It was a long, difficult night."

"My word!" Rich exclaimed. "Are you all right?"

"I got lucky. Thankfully, I am." Not that she looked the least bit all right. Makeup covered the bruise on her cheek, but her deepest wounds were on the inside. It wasn't unexpected that she didn't get into details; still it surprised him how much she downplayed what had happened. She'd come close to being killed. Not to mention there might very well be a serial killer stalking her. "I ended up staying at Nash's place and overslept. It was the first time I've had more than a few hours of solid rest in weeks."

"Is there anything I can do?" Rich asked. "Would you like me to spend the day here while you see your clients? The place feels a bit creepy when I'm in there alone these days. I can only imagine what it's like for you."

A look of embarrassment crossed her face, and she hung her head. "That's kind of you, but no. I don't have any clients coming in today. I came to see you off and to get the keys. I'm only hanging out until Yvonne drives down. Then we're off on our vacation."

"Oh, I forgot about that. I guess starting today it's a vacation for both of us. Only mine is permanent." Rich exhaled heavily.

Lynn put a hand on his good shoulder. "I'm sorry for how things turned out," she said, and Nash saw the weight she was carrying, how she blamed herself for everything surrounding Andy Crombie. "But you're making the right choice."

Nodding, Rich took a deep breath. He opened his door, slipped into the car and waved to them.

"It seems like this wasn't an easy decision for him," Nash said.

"No, it wasn't." Lynn turned, heading for the

building. "He agonized over what to do. In the end, he made the right choice. This is the best thing for him. He gets to start the next chapter of his life in sunny California, close to his family."

As they entered the building, Lynn faltered to a stop and stiffened.

He put a hand on her arm. To remind her she wasn't alone. That he was there, ready to help in any way.

"I'm fine." She nodded as if trying to convince herself. "Really, I'm fine."

"Sure."

"Is it okay if we talk in my office, instead of the waiting room?"

She was in charge of how this happened. Not him. "Yep."

He flipped the latch on the front door, locking it since she wasn't expecting any clients and Yvonne wouldn't arrive until later. Then he followed her down the hall.

"Could you write down for me where you're going to be staying with Yvonne?" They were no longer a couple, and she had every right to refuse, but it would put his mind at ease.

"I'll be fine out of town. Safer than staying here."

He hoped that was true. "Still, if you wouldn't mind and call me, too, once you get there."

"Sure," she said reluctantly.

Lynn unlocked the door and traipsed inside, taking off her coat.

Entering her office, he realized how remarkable she was. Day after day she came back here and did her job regardless of how challenging it might be for her. Rich was retiring while Lynn was sticking it out, choosing to sacrifice her personal comfort to help others. He admired her so much he didn't have the words for it.

As she grabbed a notepad and pen and looked up something on her phone, he realized there were also things about her that he couldn't wrap his head around. For instance, how she could return to a place where she'd been the most vulnerable without any protection.

"Where's the gun I gave you?" he asked. Better to cut straight to it, push through the messy bits, and hopefully find a way back to each other.

Sighing, she set down the pad and pen and leaned against the edge of her desk. "I don't carry it anymore."

"Heard that part last night." He removed his jacket, tossing it into a chair. "Why?"

Lynn clasped her hands in her lap. "You won't understand."

She was probably right.

He looked around her office, his gaze going to the Sierra Club calendar, her Ivy League degree hanging on the wall, the Montblanc pen on her desk that cost as much as her designer handbag.

The differences between them were stark. Growing up in a big city, with well-to-do parents, she had wanted for nothing. While he had lived on his family's ranch under his father's iron fist until he was thrown into the foster care system, where he learned to fight for everything if he wanted to have anything.

Sure, there were times he didn't get her perspective, her preferences. But it was their differences as much as their similarities—love of family, a strong work ethic, service before self—that attracted him to her.

"After what you went through here, I would've sworn you'd be inclined to carry it."

"It's because of what happened that I don't," she said.

"Having that gun saved your life."

"With that gun, I took a life." Her expression was determined, but she didn't look the least bit tough.

"You had no choice. Andy Crombie was going to shoot you. He was crazy."

"Don't use that word with me," she said, wagging a finger at him. "Not ever. Andy wasn't some violent criminal. He was suffering from severe mental illness. He was in crisis and needed help. It was my job to protect him." Shadows swam in her eyes, and he saw the scar that night had left. A scar that marred the soul rather than the body.

"Instead, I failed him." The self-condemnation in her voice ripped at Nash's guts.

Why couldn't she see that she had been in an impossible situation?

"If you hadn't shot him," he said, slowly, carefully, "you'd be dead."

"You don't know that for certain, but the conclusion you jump to is that killing him was the right thing."

"Why would you say that?"

"Taking a life sometimes comes with the territory of your job. I get that, but I think you might've gotten to a point where you've normalized it, so you don't feel the gravity anymore."

Is that what she thought of him? That he didn't feel the gravity of taking a life?

"You should know better than that about law enforcement." He crossed his arms over his chest. "Your brother is an FBI agent the same as me."

"I'm not talking about all law enforcement. I'm talking about you."

He swallowed, stricken, not knowing what to say. How to defend against such an accusation. He opted for his default setting, silence.

"Jake isn't like you," she said, mentioning her brother, who worked down in Denver. "Or maybe it's that I know him so much better. I've seen how deeply things affect him."

Clenching his jaw, Nash breathed through it.

This unfair comparison of him to someone she'd known and loved her whole life.

Again, his instinct was to stay quiet, but that was how the conversation had turned out before. One-sided and not going in his favor.

"Give me time." He pushed down the frustration and the ugly sense of desperation swelling in his chest. "To show you."

"Once Jake found out we were dating, he told me some things about you."

And that unfair scale tipped even further against him.

Nash cleared his throat. "What things?"

"That you consistently get the job done. No matter how tough," she said, but the compliment had him bracing for what was to come next. Lynn liked to soften the blow of the bad by starting out with something good. "That you have a reputation for being decisive…to the point of unfeeling. That you've been reprimanded for using excessive force."

His brain snagged on the one word ringing in his ears. *Unfeeling.*

For some reason, this felt like a betrayal by one of his own. He and Jake weren't friends. Still, on something like this he'd expected the guy to have his back. Not stab him in it. They were colleagues after all, working in a dangerous line of work that required tough choices.

Lynn pushed off the desk and eased closer to

him. "I didn't break up with you because of what Jake said. I form my own opinions, but it did make me look closer. Then there was the incident when you got hurt in the line of duty and a suspect died."

The man had been a violent repeat offender and had attacked Nash, resisting arrest with a deadly weapon. They'd fought on the roof of a building. The guy had gone over the edge. An accident.

If he could've brought the guy in alive, he would've.

"You wouldn't talk to me about it." Lynn's gaze lingered on him, her eyes searching his for he didn't know what. "You shut down whenever I brought it up, or anything deep for that matter. You've never even said more than ten words to me about your childhood."

"Try living your entire life keeping your thoughts to yourself, your feelings bottled up, and then one day being asked to spill your guts on demand about everything."

Served him right for falling for a therapist. When they'd met at Delgado's, he hadn't known what she was. A keep-your-distance, avoid-at-all-costs shrink. That was a headache he didn't need. He had intimacy issues, possibly trust issues, too. But there had been something about her, right from the get-go, that had hooked him.

"I found it alarming the way you'd withdraw

from me," she said, "when all I wanted was to get closer to you. Quite frankly, it scared me."

"You fear me?" He rubbed his forehead. This kept getting worse. For months, his woman had been scared of him. No wonder she'd ended things.

"I don't fear you, Nash. I fear *for* you." She closed the gap between them and put her hand on his chest.

He flinched at the contact. Not because he didn't want her to touch him. On the contrary, he wanted it too much. He ached for her. Weeks of hoping they'd work it out, and now she was touching him, yet at the same time, keeping him at a distance.

"I can't be with someone who won't talk to me," she said. "Who hides their past and their emotions. I told you it was a deal breaker and you didn't care."

It wasn't that he didn't care. "Compared to everything else going on," he said, thinking about his job, putting away criminals, "it didn't seem like a big deal." He watched a different kind of pain fill her eyes, and he regretted the words. "I mean I thought I had more time to work on it."

"Maybe we view everything too differently. Take the situation with Andy. I read the police report. You were in the process of identifying yourself when I pulled the trigger. If I had waited, ten seconds, maybe just two, then I might've registered that you were there. You might've been able to talk him down. How can you, of all people, say I didn't have any other option?"

How could he say anything else?

To do so would condemn her to live with this guilt for the rest of her life. It wouldn't be right. Not after what Andy had done, shooting Rich and turning the gun on Lynn.

Nash wanted to protect her, wanted her to heal and move on. Not suffer.

"Everything happened really fast," he said. "You could've been gone in the blink of an eye. Sometimes the only choice is the hardest one, and you have to forgive yourself for it."

"That's easier said than done."

He could help her through this. If only she'd let him. "Why have you been avoiding me?"

"Because when I listen to your voice messages," she said, "when I see you in the street, the first thing I think of is Andy. I think of what I did, and I can't bear it."

He turned, putting his back to her.

It would've been easy to leave the conversation there, with their relationship diminished to nothing more than friendship, and her stuck, unable to forgive herself.

Nash never chose easy. He was a fighter. Born and bred. He spun back around, meeting her tortured gaze. "Did you ever stop to ask yourself what's the second thing you think of when you see me? Or the third? I refuse to believe it's all death and darkness." Her amber eyes softened. Big, liquid eyes you'd see on a fawn. The same way she had softened in his truck earlier. On some level, she wanted to be near him, to get closer, and if he had kissed her, he was willing to bet everything he owned that she would've kissed him back. "You must think of Andy when you're in this office. But you still come here, every day. You haven't run from your job. Don't run from me, either."

"Continuing to work here has been a serious struggle. I've been thinking about moving back home to Fort Collins."

The statement hit him like a physical blow, and he stilled.

"My family thinks it would be good for me to go back, now that Aunt Miriam is settled in a nice place, like Silver Springs, and Delgado's is thriving. But I have an obligation to the Turning Point clients. I can't simply abandon them."

What about abandoning him?

"Running down the street to get away from me isn't good enough. You have to leave the state?"

"It's only a forty-five-minute drive."

He clasped her shoulders, and she stared up at him. "I think you've been avoiding me to punish yourself. When we're together, it's like we're in this bubble, where the outside world disappears. You said yourself that being at my place helped you get the first decent night's sleep in weeks. It's okay to be with me. To let me hold you. It's okay to feel better."

"I'm not sure I'll ever feel better here. In Laramie."

"Why not?"

Tears welled in her eyes as she lowered her head. "Because of the letters I keep getting. I don't think they'll ever stop coming unless I leave."

"What letters?"

Chapter Nine

Tension coiled so tight through Lynn she could barely breathe. She pulled out the letters from her desk drawer and gave the bundle of them to Nash with a shaking hand. "They're in chronological order. The most recent one I received was yesterday." On a wave of nausea, she sank into her leather chair and dropped her head into her hands.

This was humiliating. Being reduced to a trembling heap. Forced to drag Nash deeper into her troubles, after doing her best to cut him out of her life. He might be the only one capable of keeping her alive through this.

The panic that lived beneath her skin, burned through to the surface, paralyzing her where she sat. A tremor racked her entire body.

Five weeks ago, Sheriff Clark had done her a kindness by keeping most of the details of what had happened to Andy quiet, issuing a simple statement to the media. A nosy reporter, dissatisfied with the lack of information and sensing a story, kept digging. The day she returned to Laramie from Fort Collins a sensational article broke, announcing to everyone that she had shot Andy Crombie. The words *self-defense* had not been used, though subtly implied, right along with a dereliction of duty on her part. That as a therapist she had been culpably inefficient.

Four days later the first letter arrived. It had been a total blindside.

Her mind stumbled over images of it. She remembered the message vividly.

She had them all memorized, down to the disturbing fonts.

**YOU WERE TRUSTED AND
VIOLATED
THAT SACRED CONVENANT
IN THE WORST WAY IMAGINABLE.**

The second was equally unnerving.

**HOW CAN YOU LOOK AT
YOURSELF
IN THE MIRROR?
HOW CAN YOU SLEEP AT NIGHT
AFTER WHAT
YOU'VE DONE?**

Every time a new one appeared in the mail, she wanted to retch. She considered burning it. Never opening it. Tearing it to shreds instead of reading it. But each time she'd been compelled to see what horrible, nasty things the note would say.

YOU SHOULD BE ASHAMED.
WHERE IS YOUR HANGDOG FACE?
MAYBE YOU SHOULD JUST
HANG.

Then she became scared. Terrified that maybe someone wanted to do more than shame her. Perhaps hurt her.

YOU HAVE BECOME DEATH, THE
DESTROYER OF WORLDS.
SOMEONE SHOULD STOP YOU.

Or kill her.

YOUR TIME IS AT HAND. BUT
WHICH WILL GET YOU FIRST?
KARMA? OR ME?
BELIEVE.
YOU'LL GET WHAT YOU DESERVE!

Dread slithered over her at recalling the harsh words, so cruel and insidious.

The police had given her sympathetic looks when she'd shown them the letters but had done nothing. If they couldn't help, then no one could.

But Nash would do his best to try, using all the tools in his box. Ironically, some of the qualities that made an effective FBI agent were also the same characteristics that had eroded their relationship, driving her to end things.

She looked up at him.

There was a sharp intelligence in those gray eyes that missed little. He studied the letters with a silent, deliberate resolve.

When he had suggested that she was avoiding him to punish herself, she had thought the idea ridiculous.

Nightmares plagued her. Guilt was consuming her. Someone was terrorizing her with those cringe-inducing letters. The one man who'd ever brought her solace had become a constant reminder of her biggest regret. As if that weren't enough, now a serial killer was targeting her.

She didn't need to punish herself, not when the universe was doing such an excellent job of it. Was karma giving her what she deserved?

Staring at Nash as he examined those wretched notes gave her a surprising sense of hope that had her reconsidering his suggestion.

He looked up, his eyes flashing to hers, making her skin tingle and her heart twinge.

Besides his good looks and muscular build, there was something about him that she couldn't ignore. An aura of strength and determination, like he'd find a way to tackle any problem. Whatever it was, a little kick of awareness shot through her whenever she sensed his eyes on her.

Although her first thought when she looked at

him was of Andy, Nash was right that it most certainly wasn't the only one. Part of her had longed to escape all of this with him in their bubble. He still owned her heart, and she didn't know what to do about it. Legitimate excuses always arose as to why she needed to keep her distance—like she'd only be encouraging the unhealthy habit they'd formed, and sex wasn't going to get him to open up, really let her in the way she had always hoped he would—but perhaps he had realized something she had missed.

That she was punishing herself by pushing him away. Because deep down she knew that in his arms she might find some absolution.

Even if it was only temporary.

GRITTING HIS TEETH, Nash fumed over the letters. There was no way he could imagine the toll they were taking on Lynn, and he wasn't going to pretend to. "I'm sorry someone has been harassing you like this."

One more form of torture she didn't need.

Not only was Lynn as beautiful on the inside as she was on the outside, but she also had a powerful intellect and even more powerful compassionate spirit. It burned his gut that someone would have the vicious audacity to send her such heinous letters.

Lynn had been wise to save them, keeping each in a separate plastic resealable bag along with the envelopes. It would preserve any possible finger-prints while minimizing the addition of others.

"Have you taken these to the sheriff's office?" He doubted it because surely Holden would've told him about it, but he needed to ask.

"No. But I did take them to the Laramie PD. There was nothing they could do about it until something happened as a result."

"Why'd you go there instead of the sheriff's?"

She stared up at him and frowned. There was no need for her to say it. Because she hadn't wanted him to find out what was going on.

"Right." He set the letters down on the desk, side by side, in the order she'd received them.

All printed on the same plain white sheets. No watermarks. Nothing special about them in terms of thickness or weight to distinguish the pages from regular printing paper. The ominous words had been typed in different fonts and sizes. All of them in bold letters, all caps.

A letter sent snail mail was fairly old-school for the twenty-first century. Then again, email was a lot easier to trace if you didn't know what you were doing.

First thing first, he was going to have the notes checked for prints. He looked over the envelopes again.

"What is it?" she asked. "Did you notice something?"

"The postmarks vary in terms of location. They

were all mailed from different post offices. The first in Jackson, next Riverton, Casper, then Cheyenne. The last one was here."

"Does it mean something? Is there a pattern of some kind?"

Taking out his cell phone, he pulled up a map. He had his suspicions but wanted to be sure. "Jackson is the farthest away. Then each location draws closer to Laramie if you look at it, taking Route 26 to I-25 over to I-80." He turned his phone so she could see the screen and pointed out the route.

"What do you think it means that the last one was postmarked here?"

"I'm not sure yet." It wasn't a good thing, but he didn't need to pile more stress on her. "There are a lot of moving pieces to consider."

Lynn stood and came around the desk to where he was. "Tell me what you're thinking. Please. You've got that look in your eye."

"And what look is that?"

"The one where I can tell that you've flipped that switch in your head. Everything personal gets locked away in a vault and you disconnect. It's only stone-cold business."

Pushing everything else to the side so he could focus with a clear head was how he performed at his best. Over the years, he'd learned to suppress his personal feelings while working a case. One of his greatest strengths was his complete control over his emotions. It had served him well. But now it was impossible to disconnect, as she called it, since this concerned her.

"Don't sugarcoat it," Lynn prodded when he remained silent. "Just give it to me straight."

"It's possible that you might have more than one problem to contend with. Based on the marking Holden found on your bumper, it looks like the guy in your car last night is the TRK serial killer."

He'd given it a great deal of thought last night as he read over old news articles. Each of the three victims in Colorado had been single females, between the ages of twenty-five and thirty-five, who had stood out publicly in some way. One had been given an award for community service. Another had won a special scholarship for excellence in STEM for a master's program. The last victim had been the focus of a scandal surrounding embezzlement of company funds.

Lynn fit the profile down to the unflattering article that had been printed about her. Each had even made ATM withdrawals the night of their murder. The FBI believed it was the killer's way of psychologically tormenting the women before he moved on to the physical aspects.

After the women had been tortured and raped, they were stabbed to death. Never shot. Maybe TRK only used a gun to intimidate and coerce.

Nash had to wait until he got into the office to read over the details that hadn't been released to the media. His boss planned to update the Denver field office regarding what happened to Lynn and see if they had any new information. He also thought that Special Agent Becca Hammond might be useful providing support on this. Nash didn't have a problem with any assistance, so long as no one got in his way.

"As far as I'm aware," he continued, "TRK didn't send letters to his victims beforehand. Which means a different person, one with a grudge against you, wrote them. Mailing them from different post offices, moving strategically closer, could indicate they are preparing to take action." Almost like a countdown. "Or at least they want you to think that they are. Perhaps to scare you."

It was one horrendous thing after another for Lynn, but something about this bothered him beyond the fact that she was the target.

The letters combined with the assault last night could be a coincidence. A big one, possibly where the article about Lynn had set two different things in motion around the same time.

He believed in coincidences. They happened every day. The trick was being able to discern when something was more than coincidence.

"Well, it's working." She exhaled a shaky breath. "I'm downright terrified." Trembling, she wrapped her arms around herself protectively and cast a despondent look at him.

If he were working a case, this was where he'd step away, giving the civilian space to emotionally gather themself.

Although Lynn needed him to do his job, she also needed the things she'd asked for from him in the past.

Nash reached out and brought Lynn close, pressing her to his chest. She shivered harder, burying her face in the crook of his neck and slipping her arms around him. Caressing a hand up and down her back, he vowed to find a way to keep her safe.

"You're going to be okay. I won't let anyone hurt you."

Part of him was glad Lynn was leaving town for a few days and wouldn't be alone. He needed her safely out of the way so he wouldn't be distracted worrying about her.

Before she headed out of town, he did have a few questions for her, but it was probably best for him to wait until he showed Holden the letters. That way she wouldn't have to go through it twice.

His cell phone rang.

They pulled apart. She wiped at her eyes as he took his phone from his pocket. The number was to the sheriff's office, Holden's extension.

They must be on the same wavelength.

"Hey," Nash said. He'd spoken to Holden earlier that morning to coordinate. While Nash was with Lynn, Holden was going to begin investigating. "Did you find anything?"

"As a matter of fact, I did. You and Lynn should both get over here as soon as possible."

HOLDEN WAS EAGER to share what he'd discovered. As soon as Nash and Lynn arrived, he beckoned to them through the glass window of the chief deputy's office that overlooked the reception area.

"How are you feeling today, Lynn?" he asked as they entered the office.

"As well as can be expected, I suppose."

The two removed their coats and were about to sit.

"Actually," Holden said, "why don't you come around the desk. I've got something to show you."

Nash came to his right side and Lynn over to his left.

"After you mentioned that TRK surveilled his victims for days before striking—" he said to Nash, and a small gasp from Lynn cut him short.

Her face was pale and pinched.

Immediately Holden realized Nash had neglected to tell her, most likely due to its alarming nature, but he hadn't been told to censor anything. "Sorry about that." He looked from Lynn to Nash on guidance about how to proceed. He didn't want to step on any toes.

"It might be better if you got a cup of coffee,"

Nash said, "while I go over this stuff with Holden. Most of it will be boring."

Lynn straightened. Pushing her long brown hair behind one ear, she turned on him. "Do you think I'm too weak to handle this?"

"No." A nerve pulsed in Nash's jaw.

"Then why is this the first I'm hearing about this?"

Nash shoved his hands in his pockets. "It's just that you've already been through so much. I thought it best to do whatever I could to lessen the strain."

"I was shocked to hear that a serial killer has been watching me for days, but that doesn't mean I need to be protected from the truth." Strength flowed in her voice and gleamed in her eyes. "I need to hear everything. I'm staying."

Holden braced for Nash's response. His buddy tended to take a hard stance when he believed his actions were in the right. Considering they were talking about protecting Lynn from troubling information, he expected Nash to double down.

"You heard the lady," Nash said. "Let's get on with it."

That was surprisingly easy, but Holden wasn't complaining. He gave a curt nod. "As I was saying, Lynn mentioned that she'd left USD the same as she had every Thursday. I figured the guy might have been captured on camera while learning her routine." The good news was the grocery store had an outdoor camera mounted on the southwest corner of the building trained on the parking lot. He typed on his keyboard and brought up the security camera footage he'd obtained earlier from the store. "First, I looked at last night's feed to see when he got into her car, so I had something to go on to identify him."

He hit Play.

The video showed Lynn pulling into the lot and parking. She grabbed her stuff, got out, locking the door as the lights flashed, and hurried off to her class.

"There," Holden said, pointing at the screen. "Watch." Seconds later a man with a dark hood pulled over his head, dressed in dark clothing but without a big, bulky coat, as if to stay light and limber, strolled past the lot and headed in the same direction. The use of a winter vest and lack of a heavy winter coat made him stick out. "How long would you say to walk to USD?" he asked, pausing the video.

Lynn shrugged. "I don't know. Six to seven minutes."

"Four and a half," Nash said.

That was eerily precise.

"Note the time." He restarted the footage and fast-forwarded to the part he wanted them to see. "Less than ten minutes later, the same guy is back. Long enough for him to make sure you went inside USD and return to the lot."

"Why is he lurking in that corner?" Lynn asked.

The man stood in the shadows observing his surroundings.

"To stay out of the direct view of the camera," Holden explained. "Unfortunately, in every shot of him we can't see his face clearly but can tell he's not yet wearing the ski mask you described." Her assailant had shielded himself, either by luck or by intention. After rewinding and replaying the clip on the computer umpteen times, Holden banked on the latter. "All we know about his identity so far is that he's a white male, six foot, medium build. Any hits we might get in the database on his DNA will take a little time."

Lynn leaned in toward the screen. "What is he doing? Why is he just standing there?"

"Waiting for the lot to clear of foot traffic," Nash said. "So no one will notice him when he breaks into your car."

As soon as the lot was clear, with no one walking to the store or their car, the man leaped into action. He moved quickly, purposefully straight to Lynn's car. Taking out a slim jim, a universal lockout tool, he looked around, ensuring the coast was still clear. He used the tool to jimmy open the door.

Lights flashed on the car and the alarm must've sounded.

The man slipped inside the front seat. He bent

over, disabling the alarm, and the lights stopped flashing. Then he climbed into the back seat.

"Goodness," Lynn said, sounding astonished. "I had no idea it could be done so fast, so easily."

Provided you knew what you were doing, it was shockingly simple. People were more vulnerable than they realized, particularly if they drove an older model that lacked a decent anti-theft system.

It was a good thing Lynn's car was totaled. Knowing her, the next one would be an upgrade in terms of it being something new. Some of the latest modern cars were almost impossible to steal.

"So, he stayed cramped in my back seat for almost an hour?"

Holden nodded. "Sure did." Incredible patience. "This was a week ago." He rewound the footage back to the previous Thursday and hit Play again once Lynn's vehicle came into view. "Same guy appears." Holden pointed. "He never parks in the grocery store lot. Must be somewhere down the street, but I couldn't find any cameras that might have picked him up. This time, he doesn't return until you do." He advanced the footage, showing them.

"What do you think he was doing while I was in class?" Lynn asked.

"Watching," Nash said. "From someplace that allowed him to keep an eye on you."

Holden nodded in agreement. "My thoughts precisely. I checked security cam footage and caught him going into the coffee shop across the street."

"That's more good news. The angle of the camera in there would cover the registers as well as most of the shop."

"It does," Holden said, in a flat tone.

"But?" Nash said, waiting for the other shoe to drop.

"They suffered a power outage a couple of days ago that wiped their stored security footage."

"Do you think that's a coincidence?" Lynn asked. "Or do you think he had something to do with it?"

"My guess is that he was covering his tracks," Holden said.

"This guy is meticulous." Nash's gaze bored into his. He didn't like this scenario, and Holden understood why.

One, it suggested that the assailant was a thorough planner who was thinking two to three steps ahead. Better to have a hothead, someone who acted impulsively. That type was far easier to catch. Two, it suggested that the guy could still be out there, watching and waiting for his next opportunity since he'd gone to the trouble of covering his tracks.

"I hate this." Nash took off his Stetson and raked a hand through his hair before putting it back on.

Holden hated it, too. Lynn had come very close,

within a razor's edge, of losing her life last night. And they were no closer to neutralizing the threat.

"There's more," Nash said. He took out resealable bags that contained what appeared to be correspondence and set it on the desk. "Someone has been sending these to Lynn over the past several weeks."

Holden perused them while Nash explained what he'd ascertained thus far. The third letter made his gut clench, and it only got worse from there.

"Do you know anyone who might have a grudge against you over what happened with Crombie?" Nash asked her.

"Enough to send those dreadful letters?" She shook her head. "But it could be anybody from Jackson to Laramie."

"My gut says it's closer to home," Nash said.

"Best place to start looking," Holden agreed, "and then widen our search from there."

Lynn crossed the room and sat in one of the two chairs facing the desk. "The reason I left town for Fort Collins weeks ago for a few days was because Mrs. Crombie tracked me down at Delgado's. She screamed at me. Said horrible things. She even threw a glass of water in my face."

Holden leaned forward. "Mrs. Crombie was initially quite vocal around town about her feelings toward you." The woman had just lost a son and was grieving. She had needed someone to blame. Lynn fit the bill. "But after that news article came out," he said, and Lynn cringed, "she seemed satisfied."

She had stopped ranting and raving to anyone who'd listen, stayed home, stayed quiet.

"Or perhaps justified. To continue in a more vicious way," Nash suggested. "With those letters."

Holden glanced down at them again. His heart went out to Lynn. "Only one way to find out." He stood and put on his jacket.

"I'm coming with you," Nash said, then he turned to Lynn. "I'll grab the bag you packed from the truck. Call Yvonne. Have her pick you up here. Don't leave. Don't forget to write down your travel details and don't go anywhere alone. Got it?"

Lynn nodded. "I understand."

Chapter Ten

On the drive, Nash couldn't stop worrying about Lynn.

TRK had attacked his previous victims while they were unsuspecting and alone. Lynn was no longer either, and she was leaving town. The methodical killer presumably had opportunities to corner the women at their homes, or even to strike while they had slept. Instead, TRK had always waited until the women were in public, where they thought they were safe, to show them otherwise.

All those things should've lessened Nash's concern, but it did nothing to bring him peace of mind.

As they pulled up to the Crombie property, Nash wished he'd driven his truck to give him a better sense of control over the situation. On most cases, he preferred to work alone, do things his way. At Holden's suggestion, they'd taken his sheriff's vehicle to eliminate any confusion on the part of the Crombies as to the nature of the visit.

Holden pulled up the driveway and parked in front of the one-story log house that sat on ten acres of land on the outskirts of town. The place had gorgeous views but looked as if it was in much need of repairs.

"Let me do most of the talking in there," Holden said, killing the engine.

"Why is that?" Nash asked as they climbed out of the vehicle and headed for the house.

"Shirley Crombie is not what I'd call a pleasant woman. This is a sensitive area for her, as well as for you. A cooler head asking the questions might be prudent."

The curtains moved aside in one of the front windows. Someone was watching them. From the way the light hit the window, casting shadows, it was impossible to discern male or female.

Nash got his badge ready to show, moving it from his back pocket to one in his coat. "I'm capable of conducting an investigation that centers on Lynn."

They walked up the porch steps. The wood groaned beneath their weight.

"This isn't a matter of capability," Holden said. "Only practicality."

"Fine." He'd do his best to let Holden take the lead, but he'd step in if and when he felt it necessary.

Holden opened the screen door and knocked. "Albany County Sheriff's Department."

There was movement inside, close by. Something heavy was set down on the floor near the doorjamb. Possibly a shotgun.

The door opened. A woman in her late sixties or early seventies with weathered skin covered in liver spots and scraggly white hair framing her face stood in the doorway. She was slim but with a sturdy look about her. "What do you want?"

"Afternoon, ma'am." Holden tipped his hat at her. "I'm Chief Deputy Powell and this is Special Agent Garner."

Nash flashed his badge, giving her a chance to properly see it.

"We'd like to ask you a few questions," Holden said.

Her gaze bounced between them. "About what?"

"Do you mind if we step inside out of the cold?" Holden asked.

"As a matter of fact, I do." She closed the front of her sweater and folded her arms.

Most folks would've been more hospitable, inviting them in, offering them a cup of coffee.

Not Mrs. Crombie.

Nash took a step to the side for a better view inside the doorway on the other side of her. He glimpsed the distinctive outline of a double-barrel shotgun.

Catching Nash's eye, Mrs. Crombie leaned forward, snatched the screen door and slammed it shut. "Ask your questions right here."

"All right, ma'am." Holden took out his pad and a pen. "When was the last time you've seen Dr. Lynn Delgado?"

"I don't know. I suppose it was when I threw water in her no-good face over at Delgado's."

"I imagine you must still harbor a lot of resentment toward her," Holden said.

"Then you imagine correct. What's this about? Did something happen to her? Did she get her just deserts?"

As if the self-inflicted suffering Lynn was putting herself through wasn't enough.

"Do you wish her any ill will?" Nash asked, unable to stay silent.

Holden sighed heavily and flashed him an annoyed glance, making his disapproval known.

In a relationship, keeping quiet was no problem, but Nash wasn't used to sitting on the sidelines when it came to working a case. Holden was reminding him why he preferred to work alone, without interference or judgment, like he was getting now.

Mrs. Crombie cocked a bitter, lopsided grin. "I wish someone would blow a hole in her the way she did my boy. Do you consider that ill will?"

Nash clenched his hand, keeping it at his side. "Yes, ma'am, I do."

She sucked her teeth. "I don't turn the other cheek. I believe in an eye for an eye."

"Would you take it upon yourself to carry out such judgment?" Holden asked.

"Please." She waved a wrinkled hand at them. "If I was going to do it, it would've already been done. Before my boy was cold in the ground. First, that woman ruined the life of my oldest and then took the life of my youngest. Shameful, I tell you." Mrs. Crombie sneered. "And shame on both of you for coming here, disturbing my peace about her."

"Who's your eldest?" Nash asked.

"Phil."

"Philip Pace," Holden clarified.

"He's the only good thing to come from my first marriage," she said. "But I wouldn't let those boys call each other half brothers. No sirree. Blood is blood. And they loved each other. Phil tried to warn Andy about that Delgado woman after what happened to Phil. Andy should've listened to his big brother."

Nash braced against a gust of frigid wind. "What happened to Phil?"

"The court ordered him to take mandatory anger management classes with her as a condition of his bail. Twelve one-hour sessions. As if he needed even one. He wanted to get through it faster. Double up in a week. Dr. Delgado told him no. Then when he missed a couple of classes, she reported him to the court. Phil begged her not to. He swore he'd make it up. But she did it anyway. The court threw Phil in jail for a month. Because of her, being so cold-blooded, he missed the start of a great new job and the beginning of a semester of classes over at LCCC," she said, referring to the Laramie County Community College. "To make matters worse, the court told him that he was going to have to start those pointless classes all over again from the start. Can you believe that?"

"Why was he ordered to anger management in the first place?" Nash asked.

"Phil got into a bar fight. Broke someone's jaw. Boys are going to be boys."

"That wasn't his first offense if the court was making him take classes," Holden said.

"He's got a little bit of a temper. That's true," she said with a nod. "Got it from his father. Not his fault."

Nash bet that Shirley Crombie was the kind of mother who absolved her sons of their responsibilities as citizens, as decent people, and rushed to bail them out of difficult situations rather than holding them accountable. Such actions would only make a person worse, not better.

Behind Mrs. Crombie, a man, slightly older than her, in his midseventies, plodded by, slowing as he peered their way to see who was at the door.

"Mr. Crombie," Holden called out, with a wave, "can we speak with you for a minute?"

"He don't got nothing to say to you. Either of you." She looked over her shoulder at him. "Go watch your program, George. I'm handling this. Go on."

The old man kept shuffling forward, disappearing out of sight.

"Where can we find Phil?" Nash asked.

"Beats me," she said with a shrug. "Have you tried his apartment?"

"I doubt he's sitting in his apartment waiting for us to arrest him," Holden said. "When was the last time you saw him?"

"After the court issued a warrant for his arrest for not taking those classes all over again." She rolled her eyes. "Since then, we haven't seen hide nor hair of him."

Holden wrote in his notebook. "When? What month? What day?"

"I don't remember the day. It was sometime back in October."

Around the same time something or someone had set Andy off.

The TV blared to life in the next room.

"Turn it down!" she called out, spinning around. "George! It's too loud! I can barely hear myself think." The volume lowered. "He needs to watch his shows. Loves his daily programs. Probably more than he loves me."

For some reason, that wasn't hard to believe.

"Do you have any relatives around here Phil might turn to for assistance?" Holden asked.

"Not no more. My kin's gone. George doesn't have anybody else. Phil's father, Terry, has people in Idaho, but we don't talk to them."

"What about family friends?" Holden asked.

"Nope."

Nash gritted his teeth, his patience beginning to wear thin. "Do you know anyone in Jackson, Cheyenne, maybe Riverton or Casper?"

She shook her head. "We don't know nobody in any of those places. We've done for ourselves. Relied on ourselves. We don't need nobody else," she said with pride.

"Have you sent Dr. Delgado any harassing letters?" Nash asked.

"Letters?" A perplexed look crossed her face like she genuinely had no idea what he was talking about. "Why would I waste the money on a stamp to send her a letter when I can throw another glass of ice water in her face? Or better yet, a cup of piping hot coffee."

Was she sure Phil got his temper from his father? If so, the man was cursed with two sets of bad genes.

"One more thing," Nash said, "does *hangdog* mean anything to you?"

"Hang what?" She reeled back with a grimace. "Did somebody hang her dog? Is that what this is about? I would never hurt a defenseless animal."

Well, that was good to know.

"Delgado wronged this family, that's a fact, but I guarantee you we ain't the only ones she's angered. Ask around, you'll see. And if her dog got hung," she added, the features of her face contorting in a nasty expression, "and it broke her heart, made her cry for days on end, then good for her."

Grief notwithstanding, that was a spiteful woman.

"We won't take up any more of your time," Holden said. "If you hear from Phil—"

Mrs. Crombie slammed the door in their faces.

They turned into the icy wind, headed for the steps. The air was bitter cold. Snowflakes were falling heavily. The roads would be blanketed with a couple of inches within the hour.

"What do you think?" Holden asked him.

Shirley Crombie didn't have the intelligence or the patience for a snail-mail campaign. "I don't think she's behind the letters."

"Neither do I. But Phil on the other hand..." Holden gave a one-shouldered shrug. "A man who was taking classes at LCCC and has nothing except time on his hands while he's in hiding might."

"You think he'd take the risk, making the drive to Jackson and the other cities when there's a bench warrant out for him?"

"Not much risk," Holden said, "if he's doing it at two a.m. and doesn't commit any traffic violations to cause him to get pulled over. A weekly road trip to mail a threatening letter might be his only outlet."

Nash opened the car door and got in. "Mind if you focus on finding him while I concentrate on TRK?" He couldn't wait to get into the office and dig into a couple of things that had been bugging him.

"Divide and conquer sounds good." Holden hopped in. "Mrs. Crombie might be onto something about someone else in town having an axe to grind with Lynn. I'll look into it, but first, I think I need to get a warrant."

Nash climbed in and shut the cold out. "For what?"

"To search that house." He hiked his chin up at the Crombie place. "I'm pretty sure Phil is hiding in there somewhere. Like she said, they rely on themselves and don't need anyone else."

"How long to get the warrant?" Nash asked.

"All depends on the judge."

As Holden backed out of the driveway, Nash's cell phone rang. He pulled it from his pocket. The number was for the Denver field office.

"Special Agent Garner," he said, answering it.

"I would have at the very least," snapped the male voice on the other end, "expected a call from you considering this involves my sister."

Jake Delgado. Fellow agent who trash-talked his colleagues for a hobby.

"I followed procedure." Nash kept his tone level and his temper in check. He'd notified his boss late last night that Lynn appeared to be the target of TRK. His boss had said that he would update the Denver office in the morning.

"To hell with procedure. How about a little common courtesy?" Jake asked.

"If Lynn thought you needed to be notified,

she would've picked up the phone and called you herself."

"I just got off the phone with her," Jake said. "Thank goodness she's on the road, on her way out of town. Otherwise, I'd be in the car, headed there now." Denver was an easy two-and-a-half-hour drive from Laramie. "My sister gets a pass, considering she was the one who was attacked and in a car crash. It's understandable if *she* wasn't thinking clearly. But *you*? What's your excuse?"

Nash didn't need one, and he didn't bother to offer any.

"Garner, you should know better. How would you feel if it was your sister?"

He didn't have any sisters, but if this was happening to one of his brothers, he would've appreciated a phone call. In hindsight, he would've handled things differently. Not as if he needed to give Jake any additional reasons to dislike him. "I'm a little busy investigating, trying to make sure a serial killer doesn't get your sister. So if there isn't anything else—"

"I hope you're not going rogue, doing this by yourself."

"Rogue would imply that I'm breaking the rules. This might be personal, but I'm doing it by the book."

"We have partners for a reason on cases like this. I doubt you can be objective considering this involves your *ex*."

Throw salt in the wound. "Could you be objective? Would you let someone else head up the investigation?"

"I wouldn't do it alone. That's my point."

"I've coordinated with local law enforcement and I'm working with the chief deputy of the sheriff's office closely on this. My boss has also brought Special Agent Hammond up to speed." Becca was staking out Lynn's place in case TRK went there looking for her. "If I need her assistance, I've got her number on speed dial. Provided that's your only concern, let that put your mind at ease."

"When you're involved, my concerns are endless."

"I'm the first to admit that my record isn't spotless." He'd been written up for insubordination, once, as well as excessive use of force. Also a onetime offense. Never the same mistake twice. "But my success rate is above reproach." Every scumbag he'd gone after, he'd nailed.

A loud exhale on the other end of the line. "I didn't only mean professionally. Look, I don't think you're a good match for my little sister. She needs someone softhearted with a PhD or MD. Someone who's going to make her laugh and take her dancing. Not someone like you or even me, for that matter," Jake said.

As far as Nash was concerned, all of that might be true, but it was up to Lynn to decide those things for herself. "None of that is any of your business."

"You're right, and it's not important right now. My only priority is keeping her safe. Okay. I don't want anything to happen to Lola."

Hearing the nickname her family called her with such affection made Nash think how it might be true that he'd always held back in his relationship with her. For one, he had never used the moniker. To him, calling her *Lola* would've indicated he wanted to take things to the next level. Something he hadn't been ready for.

Nash took a deep breath, realizing Jake's current hostility was more about his worry for his sister than his dislike of him, the ex. Fighting with him was a waste of both their energy. "I'll do everything in my power to make sure nothing happens to her." He'd risk his life to protect hers in a heartbeat. "We're going to find this guy. And stop him. You've got my word."

Chapter Eleven

Snow fell in big, thick flakes so dense that the wipers struggled to clear arcs across the windshield. Rounding the last bend, the tires of Yvonne's four-wheel-drive scrabbled for purchase on the slick surface as the Red Tail Lodge came into view.

The log cabin sat perched on a hilltop in the Snowy Range, surrounded by the Medicine Bow-Routt National Forests. Smoke wafted from the chimney. On the front door was a modestly decorated wreath.

They pulled in front of the wide wooden staircase and came to a stop. Lynn gave a silent sigh of relief that they'd made it there safely.

"Finally," Yvonne said, sounding as relieved as Lynn felt.

They got out of the Jeep, and snow crunched underfoot. Lynn took in a deep breath of clean mountain air. Nothing in the world smelled better.

She looked around at their remote surroundings.

Clouds darkened the late-afternoon sun, bringing an early twilight. A heavy layer of snow blanketed everything, turning the landscape into a picturesque winter wonderland. The small lodge rented rustic cabins for those looking to unplug and unwind surrounded by the splendor of nature.

Down the hill behind the main house, she spotted four cabins spaced far apart to give guests their privacy.

They hurried up the steps and pushed through the front door, which had a welcome sign hanging in the middle of the wreath. The heavenly scent of cedar and pine enveloped them. An enormous Christmas tree that looked professionally decorated stood twenty feet tall beside a roaring fire. The main house was deceptively large on the inside.

They stomped off the snow from their boots on the mat before stepping onto the hardwood floors.

Wearing a faux-fur zebra-print headband, fuchsia parka that somehow didn't clash, slim-fitting winter pants that highlighted her svelte figure, and with her dark blond hair pulled into a sleek ponytail, Yvonne looked ready to hit the slopes in Aspen instead of lying low in a rustic cabin. It was a shame some hot single guy would miss seeing her in that sexy outfit.

They both headed for the front desk where a man in his seventies rose to his feet.

"Welcome to the Red Tail Lodge. You two must be Ms. Lamber and Ms. Delgado. I'm Earl Epling, the owner. Please call me Earl."

"Hello. I'm Yvonne."

"Nice to meet you. I'm Lynn."

"Glad you two made it with the storm that's rolling in."

"Storm?" Lynn asked, taking off her gloves. "I thought we were just getting some snow."

"The most recent weather report mentioned something about the pressure center shifting, becoming so low that it increased the wind and intensity of things out there, turning it into a deadly storm. Heavy snow, freezing temperatures, possible ice. But not to worry. Now that you're here, this is the best possible place to be in a storm. Your cabin has plenty of firewood and your fridge is stocked per Ms. Lamber's instructions."

"Drop the 'Ms.' Call me Yvonne." Her best friend flashed a smile at Earl. "Thank you for helping me out on that front. You saved us a trip to the grocery store."

Lynn thought it would be a horrible inconvenience to ask someone at the lodge to pick up groceries for them if they were willing to do it at all. Yvonne had disagreed. Working in hospitality, she was confident that almost any accommodation could be met, especially if you were willing to pay a little extra to make it happen.

"Not a problem," Earl said. "My son, Ryan, got everything in town. He brought it up the mountain, loaded it in your cabin and then hightailed it out of here before the storm."

"Thank you," Lynn said to the kind owner, but she also patted her friend's arm in thanks as well. Yvonne was a great planner who prepared for everything. Lynn never should've doubted the idea that had saved them time and made the start of their vacation much easier.

Easy was what she needed right now.

"We usually provide breakfast and dinner up here at the main house," Earl said, "but with it being so close to Christmas and you two being our only guests, my wife, who does all the cooking, is visiting with the kids and grandbabies. So I didn't charge you anything extra for the grocery run."

"We had no idea we were the only guests. I'm sorry we're keeping you from your family," Lynn said, hating to be an intrusion.

"Don't be silly. That's why we're here." Earl gave a smile so warm it turned his affable features ruddy. "To help folks get away from it all. There was another couple scheduled to come tomorrow, but they've pushed their arrival back a day to be sure the storm has passed and the roads have been cleared. Better safe than sorry. That's what I always say." He set a brochure down on the counter. "We've got a variety of movies and a ton of books you're free to borrow. The VHS cassettes and DVDs are all listed in there," he said, and she exchanged a look with Yvonne that screamed *who owns a VCR anymore?* "Also there's a map of trails in the area if you're interested once the storm dies down. Now I just need a credit card. Should I run the same one on file that the reservation was made under?"

"Yes, that would be fine," Yvonne said since she had booked the place.

Lynn had planned to cover half the expenses before she'd canceled all her cards after her wallet had been stolen. "I'll pay you back my share."

"Are you kidding me? Not a chance. This is my treat."

Yvonne had been horrified as Lynn had recapped everything she'd been going through on their ride up the mountain. She only wished she had shared the threatening letters sooner with Yvonne and Nash. Trying to deal with this nightmare on her own hadn't been working. She'd always considered herself a strong, independent woman, but there came a point where everyone needed help.

"Thanks," Lynn said, trying to hide her embarrassment. She'd make it up to Yvonne on her birthday next year.

Earl turned and grabbed a key from one of the hooks on the wall behind him. "You're in cabin number two. It's the first one on the right. You can drive down the hill and park in front of your cabin, if you want, but with the heavy amount of snow we're about to get, it'll be difficult to get out. I recommend leaving your vehicle parked where it is and carrying your bags down."

Yvonne sighed. "I hope you're up for a workout."

"We can handle it." They both were thirty years

old, made it a point to stay fit and had packed lightly for their five-day getaway. Both of them only had overnight bags that they could sling on their shoulders. No heavy wheeled luggage to trudge through the snow.

"Would you like snowshoes?" Earl bent down, grabbing a pair from under the counter, and held them up.

Lynn and Yvonne exchanged a questioning look, debating whether to take them.

"I think we'll pass," Yvonne said. "There's only three or four inches of snow."

"Suit yourself. If you need anything else, give me a ring," Earl said. "Your cell phones won't work around here, but the cabins have landlines."

Lynn took her phone from her pocket. There was a *no service* message in the top right corner of her screen. "What about Wi-Fi?"

"Sure, here in the main house. Afraid not in the cabins though."

When the Red Tail Lodge website had mentioned *unplugging* from the world, Lynn hadn't realized that they'd meant it literally.

"Your Honor, with all due respect, this is unacceptable." Standing in front of the massive mahogany desk that ate up most of the square footage in the judge's chambers, Holden put a fist on his hip. "I don't think you understand the urgency of the situation."

"First," Judge Don Rumpke said, lifting a finger, "when anyone prefaces a statement as you did 'with all due respect,' it means whatever follows is most assuredly not respectful." Don unzipped his black robe, hung it on a hook and put on his suit jacket. All bad signs. "Second, there is nothing wrong with my comprehension of the situation. You've simply failed to convince me of this sudden supposed urgency."

"As I've already explained, there is an outstanding bench warrant for Phil Pace. Dr. Delgado is being harassed. She's received five threatening letters, and I suspect Phil may be behind it. There's no reason to deny the warrant to search the Crombies'."

"Repeating yourself without adding any new information does nothing to persuade me." Don began packing up his briefcase. "The Crombie residence was searched by—" he paused as he leafed through some pages "—Deputy Livingston in your department when the bench warrant was first issued."

Holden must've been out that day, because he would not have let Livingston go to the Crombies' alone. Not only was Livingston constantly slipping up, making inexcusable mistakes, even for a rookie, but Shirley would've pushed him around, preventing him from doing his job properly. The new sheriff, Daniel, had still been getting to know everyone, feeling out personalities and assessing capabilities.

"Phil Pace was not found on the premises," Don continued.

"Mrs. Crombie probably assumed the house would be searched within the first forty-eight hours and that afterward they'd be in the clear. I have reason to believe that he's hiding in that house."

"I don't doubt you. Phil is most likely squirreled away in a closet somewhere. That's why I've agreed to issue the warrant *tomorrow*."

Holden gritted his teeth. "It has to be today, Your Honor. It can't wait."

"Oh, really?" Don slipped on his wool coat and put his fedora on his head. "Look outside and tell me what you see."

Holden didn't bother looking. "Snow, sir."

"Know what I see? A blizzard. That storm is going to shut down roads, knock out power for some, the unfortunate ones with no generators. Every time we get one of these major snowstorms, emergency services will get flooded with calls. Now, you're asking me to tap vital resources to search the Crombies in this." Don waved a hand toward the snowstorm outside. "If Phil is hiding somewhere in that house, as he probably has been for the past two months, he'll still be there tomorrow. He's not running out to mail any letters and make a great escape in that wicked weather. As I've said, I don't see the urgency. It can wait. As for me, I'm going home to snuggle with my wife in front of the fire and enjoy a cup of hot cocoa."

"If Phil is responsible and he does get away, this will be on your head, Your Honor. I would hate to have to file a complaint to the Commission on Judicial Conduct and Ethics. Neither of us would have to worry about it coming to that if you just issued me the warrant. Today."

"You of all people are threatening me?" Don exhaled with a look of exhaustion. "You are on thin ice as far as I'm concerned, Holden James Powell," Don said, and Holden took it as another bad sign when one's elder called them by their full name. "The previous sheriff, your boss, turned out to not only be corrupt but also in cahoots with your former fiancée." Don paused for effect, letting the wretched but truthful statement hang in the air like a bad odor. "And you claim to have had no idea."

"That's true." To his shame, when the scandal broke, he had been as shocked as everyone else, but also humiliated. How could he have not known? Had he been too trusting? Too naive?

Too obtuse?

The worst part wasn't that he'd become the laughingstock of Laramie. No, what was even worse was that it had been a bigger blow to his pride than his heart. It made him realize that he hadn't been in love. The engagement had been her idea, and he'd agreed because the relationship had been easy, effortless. Turns out that it had been without any problems, as if they were a match made in heaven, because she had been using him the entire time.

"The whole town has heard some cockamamie story of how you, Mr. Smart-as-a-Whip, were suddenly clueless when it came to the two people you were closest to, who were doing dirty business right under your nose." Don neglected to mention the fact that one of his fellow judges had been less than honorable—corrupt—and also embroiled in the scandal. "They may buy it. Part of me wants to as well because I know your parents and I know they raised you right. But had it been up to me, you would've been fired to clear out the stink from the sheriff's department and to let it have a fresh start."

The declaration was like a cold, hard slap in Holden's face.

He straightened and stood his ground. "Good thing then that it wasn't up to you."

"Be grateful you still have your position as chief deputy sheriff. Be grateful I'm going to give you your warrant. Tomorrow. Be grateful you're free to accomplish other important tasks instead of utilizing precious resources that'll be needed elsewhere," Don said.

His plate was full at the moment. He had Mitch compiling a list of other individuals enrolled in the anger management program that Lynn had been running. Once that was done, he'd have to start knocking on doors and asking questions.

"Before I leave," Don said, "I'd like to hear your gratitude, if you'd like me to sign your warrant."

Holden swallowed the anger rising in his throat. "I earned my position as chief deputy. I'm not proud of what happened with the previous sheriff and my fiancée. In fact, I'm embarrassed by it. But I didn't break the law. I've done nothing but uphold it and I deserved to keep my position." Despite what everyone in town thought to the contrary. "Thank you for your time, Your Honor. But I will no longer be needing your warrant."

Frowning, Don rocked back on his heels. "What are you going to do without it?"

"There's more than one way to skin a cat." He knew a bail bondsman itching to get his hands on Phil Pace. If Phil had listed his parents' place as an address he frequented on the bail agreement, then the bail bonds agent had statutory authority to search the premises without a warrant. Knowing Phil, not planning to jump bail, he'd put the Crombies' residence down on that agreement.

"Well, if your clever little plan falls through, I'll be here tomorrow, waiting for you to come back to me with hat in hand."

Holden hoped with every fiber of his being it wouldn't come to that. "Enjoy your cocoa and give Mrs. Rumpke my regards."

THE ONE THING niggling at the back of Nash's mind was when TRK marked Lynn's car. Living across the street from the University of Wyoming Police Department meant that the front of her house along with the garage where she kept her car were covered by security cameras. Still, he'd followed protocol and reviewed the footage to be sure he hadn't overlooked anything.

Her car hadn't been marked at her home. Of that he'd been certain.

As far as he knew, she hadn't resumed any of her volunteer activities. The only other places she went regularly were USD, Turning Point and the Silver Springs senior living center.

One phone call had given him access to the surveillance footage of the nursing home, and according to their logs, Lynn had most recently visited last Saturday, six days ago, between one and three in the afternoon.

Nash rewound the footage to twelve fifty-five. Two minutes later Lynn pulled into the lot adjacent to the living center and parked. From the way she grabbed her purse and hopped out of the vehicle, she seemed to be in a hurry. Hair hanging loose around her face and wearing a dress and heels, she walked at a brisk clip and disappeared inside.

Not long after, a man with a black hoodie over his head, same lightweight vest as worn in the previous video of the supermarket, crossed the street and entered the parking lot. His head was lowered and canted away from the camera. He was aware they were there, once again, deliberately trying to avoid getting his face captured.

Taking out a pocketknife, the man knelt at the back of Lynn's vehicle and began scraping a mark on her bumper. His head was on a constant swivel to the left and right, staying aware of his surroundings.

Nash's attention shifted across the screen. Lynn shoved through the front door of the center, headed back for her car.

But the man was still there.

She pressed the key fob and her lights flashed.

He crouched lower for a second, and, timing it just right so as not to be seen, he scurried around to the right side behind another vehicle as Lynn reached hers. She ducked inside, grabbed something from the back seat, and emerged holding a bag from the bakery that was down the street from Delgado's. Her aunt Miriam loved their pastries.

The man could've stayed low, hiding until she went back inside. Instead, the son of a gun stood, strode around the other car, pushing his hood back to reveal his face, and approached Lynn. He stopped her in the middle of the parking lot, keeping his back to the camera, and spoke to her.

A chill danced across Nash's skin watching Lynn smile and nod as she pointed to the facility. The jerk even made her laugh right before she gestured for him to come into the center.

He shook his head no and glanced at his watch.

Then he said something else to which she nodded again and waved goodbye.

Four minutes and twelve seconds. That's how long TRK had spoken to Lynn.

She'd been open and engaged, with no hint of wariness. She'd seen his face, heard his voice, laughed at his joke, invited him inside, waved to him as though...

As though TRK had passed himself off as a concerned family member contemplating putting a loved one in Silver Spring. That had to be it. The only reason Lynn wouldn't have been more guarded talking to a random stranger.

All this time he'd been tracking her, getting up close and personal, and she'd been none the wiser. But now she could identify him. With a physical description, they would be able to have a forensic artist draw an image of him. Then they could plaster his face everywhere.

Nash took out his cell and dialed Lynn. It went to voice mail without ringing.

Why would she turn off her phone? What if he needed to reach her with updates?

He tried once more. Straight to voice mail again. "Hey, Lynn. It's me. Give me a call as soon as you get this message. It's urgent."

As he disconnected, he had a bad feeling in the pit of his stomach.

This time he tried Yvonne. He still had her number saved in his contacts.

Same thing. Not a single ring, and voice mail picked up.

Maybe they had both deliberately shut off their phones for the weekend. But what were the odds of that? Lynn and Yvonne treated their phones like they were appendages. Always connected to them. One of them might have turned it off, but not both.

Cold dread was a sick knot in his gut.

There could be an acceptable explanation. Perhaps they were out of range of service.

Or…

Nash blocked the horrible thought that sprang to mind before it could sprout roots and germinate. Overreacting and jumping to the worst conclusion would get him nowhere. Only talking to Lynn would calm his fears.

He turned back to his computer to look up the number to the mountain retreat and call the front desk.

His chest tightened. The only problem was he'd never gotten the name of the place. All he knew was that it was a lodge somewhere in the state that rented cabins. He'd pressed her for the details, and she'd finally agreed to give them to him. Back at the clinic, she'd had the notepad in her hand and was about to write everything down until he had sidetracked her by getting into their relationship. Then she'd told him about the letters and had focused on the new threat.

Before heading out with Yvonne, maybe she had still written it down.

He made a quick check with Holden to see if she'd passed along anything to the people in his office, where he'd left Lynn to wait for her girlfriend.

No one had seen her leave any info for him, no notes.

He checked his phone messages. Nothing.

Had she deliberately kept it from him—was she that desperate to be out of his sphere?

Due to the theft of her wallet, he had authorization to monitor her credit cards in case the guy was stupid enough to use one. So far, he hadn't been. But that permission also allowed him to dig through recent credit card authorizations.

He brought up her transactions and perused the last two months when she would have booked the cabin.

Dead end. Yvonne must have reserved it. Getting access to her credit card transactions would require a warrant.

Tamping down anxiety, he needed to tackle this logically. There was no reason for them to drive three hours or longer. Not when there were mountain ranges offering stunning vistas so much closer to home.

Maybe she'd told Jake the name of the place when they'd spoken earlier. Not that he was looking forward to another chat with her brother.

Nash went to recent calls in his cell and dialed him.

"Agent Delgado."

"This is Nash."

An exasperated sigh. "I'm in the middle of something urgent, can this wait?"

"I'll make it quick," Nash said. "Did Lynn happen to tell you the name of the place where she's staying?"

"Um," Jake hesitated. "I thought she had, but thinking back on it, no. It's some lodge in the mountains. I was so upset about her getting attacked and neither of you calling me that I didn't focus on it."

At least Nash wasn't alone there. "Did she mention their driving time?"

"A couple of hours," Jake said, confirming Nash's best guess. "Why? Did something happen?"

"She can identify the man we're looking for, but she doesn't realize it. I found a video of him talking to her." Nash withheld the part about it happening outside of Silver Spring because he didn't want to unnecessarily upset her brother. Seeing the playback had made Nash's blood boil. "Her cell goes straight to voice mail."

"Did you try Yvonne?"

"Of course. Same thing."

"The service connection can be dodgy up in the mountains."

"Yeah, I realize. That's why I wanted to call the place. Reach her via landline. I'll make a list of the possible retreats and start checking with them."

"One sec." The line sounded muffled, like Jake had put his hand over the phone. "Hey, I've got to go. Something urgent has come up. If you haven't been able to reach her by morning, let me know."

"Sure." Nash stabbed the end call icon.

Damn it. He banged his fist on the desk in his cubicle, drawing a few looks from the others on the task force.

Drawing a breath, he faced his computer.

Beginning his search with retreats around Laramie Mountain, Medicine Bow Mountain and Snowy Range were his best bets. He'd make a list of all of them in the area and going in alphabetical order, call them one by one until he reached her.

Chapter Twelve

"This is perfect." Lynn set down the map of trails she'd been looking at and took the filled champagne flute Yvonne handed her. "Just what the doctor ordered." Her body ached all over, but she decided to forgo taking any more NSAIDs in lieu of some medicinal bubbly.

Yvonne poured a second glass of ice-cold champagne and sat on the bearskin rug beside her in front of the fire. "I can't believe we planned this vacation to distract you from the fact that it would've been your anniversary with Nash and it turned into a much-needed great escape from town. Never in a million years would I have imagined you being targeted by a homicidal maniac."

That made two of them.

Lynn hadn't mustered the courage to go into detail about the threatening letters and had kept the description of them vague. A serial killer was enough to flatten the vacay vibe. Plus, she didn't want Yvonne giving her any more pity looks.

"Speaking of which, I should probably call Nash and let him know that I got here safely."

"A little worry can do wonders to make the heart grow fonder. You're safe. You're with your bestie. Let him wait until the morning. Trust me."

Maybe Yvonne was right.

Lynn had left the details of where she was staying with Deputy Livingston. If Nash really needed to hear her voice, he'd call the Red Tail Lodge.

"So, you spent the night with Nash." Yvonne flashed a coy smile. "I want to hear all the juicy details."

Sipping her bubbly, Lynn leaned back against the sofa. "Nothing juicy to tell. I spent the night at his place. Not in his bed." Although there had been a part of her that had longed to curl up beside him, absorb his warmth, his comfort. "He only offered because he's the kind of man who does the right thing."

"Oh, please." Yvonne waved a dismissive hand at her. "He's the kind of man who'll seduce you out of your knickers given the chance." They both laughed. "There's nothing wrong with that, and yes, he's also a good guy. Very loyal *and* he likes to snuggle. That's really hard to find."

"Not if I get a dog. They're loyal and the right breed will cuddle with me."

More laughter as they clinked their glasses together.

"Seriously, I was rooting for you two," Yvonne said. "I like him. You were so relaxed around him. You always looked happy. Practically glowed around him, like you radiated joy from the inside out."

"Yeah." Lynn sighed with disappointment. "When things were good, they were the best.

But he won't talk to me. How am I supposed to know who he really is? How he feels about things? About me?" She set her glass on an end table. "The entire time we were together he never said the three words."

"I. Love. You." Yvonne's voice was singsongy and playful.

The words had slipped from Lynn's mouth one night at dinner. Nash had looked like a june bug caught in a zapper. Immediately, she'd taken it back, claiming the timing was wrong. Then he'd gotten a work call and left.

She hadn't brought it up again. Neither had he.

"Ten months," Lynn said. No declarations of love. No letting her in behind his emotional bulwark. No sharing his past. It was too much.

"I've had a lot of guys say it to me, usually after I've rocked their world in bed, and do you know how many of them meant it?" Yvonne formed a zero with her fingers. "Talk is cheap. When you were with him, did you feel loved?"

Lynn shrugged. "I think so." She had felt adored, sexy, safe. Seen, like he knew her, but she wanted to know him in the same way.

"Are you sure that he won't eventually open up under the pressure of your superhero therapist skills given enough time?"

Time was what he had asked for. "But how much?" Shouldn't she follow the same advice she gave her clients? Express your expectations. Set a deadline to see results and stick to it. She was done with dating around and was ready to settle down. Start a family. "Aren't we here to talk about anything but this?"

"I'm sorry." Yvonne topped off her glass of champagne. "You're absolutely right. How does steak and a rom-com sound?" She patted the thick stack of chunky VHS tapes on the floor next to the DVDs they'd also picked out. "Nothing sappy. Something to make us laugh out loud until our stomachs hurt."

"Sounds like you're reading my mind."

Yvonne wrapped an arm around her shoulder and pressed their temples together. "It's all going to work out. You'll see. In the meantime, I'll do my job and keep you distracted without a care in the world. I'm even going to do all the cooking. You won't have to lift a finger since you wouldn't let me take you to that magnificent ranch at Elk Creek. The one with the luxurious spa."

The ranch with cabins looked like heaven. But paradise was pricey. A hundred and fifty dollars for a manicure, three hundred for a facial, four for a massage. None of which included the cost for the cabin. She'd rather put that money toward her down payment for a house or shoes or purses. All of which would last a lot longer than a few hours of pampering.

"This is what I really needed," Lynn said. "Quality time with you away from the real world."

Not thinking about anything serious. Forgetting her troubles.

"No better way for us to continue our escapism than with a movie and more champagne."

"ARE YOU SURE there's no way I can persuade you to do it today?" Holden asked, speaking into his cell phone as he walked down the hall of the Albany County Courthouse toward the sheriff's department.

"Sorry, man. No can do," Trevor said. "I'm in Cheyenne, visiting my mother, and there is no way I'm driving back to Laramie in this weather."

Holden turned left down the next hall. "But it's Phil Pace we're talking about." Just as he'd suspected, Phil had listed the Crombie residence on the bail agreement.

"I'd love nothing more than to get my hands on that weasel and wring his neck, but I can't do it today. No one in their right mind would in this weather. I'll be back the day after tomorrow."

Two doors down another corridor, he came to the open set of double doors with Sheriff's Department stenciled on the front and waltzed inside.

"That's too late." Holden would have his warrant before then.

"I don't know what else to tell you. Sorry."

He pushed through the half door at the reception counter and acknowledged Mitch Cody with a nod. "Yep. Thanks anyway." He hung up and put away his cell.

Mitch got up from his desk and cut across the room, headed toward him.

Holding up a hand in greeting to the sheriff, who was on the phone across the hall in the larger office, Holden traipsed into his own office with Mitch close on his heels.

"Who burst your bubble?" Mitch asked.

Holden must've looked as defeated as he felt. Even his bail bondsman wasn't willing to venture out in this storm. "The Honorable Judge Don Rumpke." The judge was going to love seeing Holden with hat in hand tomorrow morning. Not wanting to rehash everything with Mitch since he'd have to do so when he updated the sheriff, he changed the subject. "What did you find?"

"I have ten names for you," Mitch said.

Jeez, that sounded like a lot. Holden had expected five, tops. He took the list from Mitch and looked it over. "Why are people divided into two columns? What's AM and DV?"

"Anger management and domestic violence."

Weren't they both about anger? "What's the difference?"

"I don't know. One's about beating up people in bars and throwing a fit at work while the other is about beating your spouse?"

"We should probably ask a professional." The distinction seemed important. He picked up the phone and called Dr. Jennings over at the Turning Point clinic. His voice mail picked up, stating that he was retiring and referring all calls to Lynn. *Great.* Holden looked up his cell phone number and tried that.

The call was answered on the second ring. "Hello."

"Dr. Jennings, this is Chief Deputy Holden Powell. I had a quick question. I'm going to put you on speaker. I have Deputy Mitch Cody with me."

"All right."

He hit the speaker button and put down the receiver. "We know Lynn was treating people in the anger management and domestic violence programs. What's the difference between the two?"

"Well, in the former, the program focuses on anger as a misunderstood and misaligned emotion, which often follows fear, depression, stress, or a perceived threat or personal attack."

"Like starting a bar fight after you feel verbally provoked or threatened?" Holden asked.

"Yes. It could even be something like a supervisor demotes someone and that person lashes out in response. Domestic violence on the other hand is about power and control. That program deals with male and female socialization, male domination, interrupting the cycle of violence. It doesn't focus on saving relationships, but rather on ending abusive and violent behavior."

"So if a husband felt that the program was a threat to his marriage," Holden said, thinking out loud, "because it might result in his wife leaving him, could he in turn view Lynn as a threat?"

"Oh, yes, definitely," Dr. Jennings said. "That's why I handed off both programs to Lynn. It was one of the conditions of her joining my practice."

Rather than taking the heat, Jennings had thrown Lynn into the fire. "Is there anyone in particular who stands out in your mind as being likely to go so far as to harass her, but anonymously?" He wasn't sure if Jennings was aware of the letters and didn't think it was a good idea to unnecessarily share that information.

"Sure," Dr. Jennings said. "Any of the people in the domestic violence program. Take your pick."

Holden stared down at the seven names in the DV column. One woman. Six men.

But only one person concerned him. Todd Burk. He belonged to a motorcycle gang called the Iron Warriors. The club had suspected ties to illicit activity. Nothing they'd been able to prove so far. At least half of the members were rotten apples, real dregs of society. Todd was one of the worst. He wasn't married but had a girlfriend who lived with him. She always refused to press charges against him, no matter how badly he had hurt her. Once Todd had beaten her in public, in front of witnesses willing to make sworn statements. Unfortunately, the corrupt judge who had been on the Iron Warriors' payroll had ordered Todd to take the domestic violence program instead of jail time.

Getting to Todd meant going through the Iron Warriors. A bridge he didn't want to have to cross.

"I also remember Phil Pace getting quite irate with Lynn one day in the waiting room," Jennings said, "because she wouldn't let him circumvent the rules of the program. He's the type who wouldn't threaten an authority figure outright and would prefer an anonymous method."

"Thank you for speaking with us, Dr. Jennings."

"Happy to help in any way that I can."

"Stay safe in this storm." Holden disconnected. The perspective was insightful, but it also brought him back to square one. He needed to find Phil Pace.

Then, if necessary, he'd talk to Todd Burk.

NASH HAD CONTACTED almost every cabin retreat within a two-hour driving range of Laramie. Twenty-two so far. Everyone he had talked to didn't have Lynn or Yvonne listed as guests. He had thought for sure the lodge at the Elk Creek Ranch with the fancy spa would have been the one he was looking for. Yoga, massages, facials and gourmet meals were right up Lynn and Yvonne's alley. But no such luck.

There were only three others left on his list.

All in the Snowy Range. The Moosehead Dude Ranch, Painted Cup Cabins and the Red Tail Lodge.

THE LANDLINE RANG in the kitchen.

Yvonne paused the '80s movie that neither of them had seen before, starring Melanie Griffith, Harrison Ford and Sigourney Weaver.

"I'll get the phone." Lynn stood and crossed the open space to the counter. Like everything else at the lodge, the phone was old school. It was lime green, attached to the wall and had a long, coiled cord. She took the receiver from the hook. "Hello."

"Is this Yvonne or Lynn?" Earl asked. His voice was tight and curt, lacking the cordial tone from earlier.

"This is Lynn. Is everything okay?"

"I need Yvonne to come up here. Her credit card didn't go through."

"Oh. We're sorry about that." Too bad Lynn didn't have one to give over the phone. She couldn't even offer a check that wouldn't bounce. "I can put her on. She probably has another one that—"

"No, no, that won't do," he said, his voice sharpening. "I need to see Yvonne right now. Have her come up to the main house to get this sorted." The line disconnected.

"How rude," Lynn said, staring at the receiver in her hand. "He hung up on me."

"What's going on?"

"Earl said your credit card didn't go through." She hung up the phone. "He wants you to come up to the main house. Apparently taking care of it over the phone isn't good enough."

"That's weird." Yvonne set down her glass, grabbed her boots that were near the fireplace and tugged them on. "There's plenty of room on the card I gave him, but sometimes my bank will decline a large charge until they've checked with me first." She picked up her cell and frowned at the screen. "Of course, they have no way of contacting me." Yvonne took her coat from the hook, slipped it on and grabbed her purse. "I might have to call to get the charge to go through. Worst case, I have another one I can use."

Lynn picked up her boots from beside the hearth. "Do you want me to come with you?"

Yvonne gave her a displeased look that warned her to stay put.

"Okay," Lynn said, raising her palms. "How about I get dinner started?"

"Only if you don't mind. I'm supposed to cook for you."

Her bestie really was the best. "It's no trouble, and I'm willing to let you do all the cooking tomorrow."

Yvonne opened the door, the old wood groaning on the hinges, as she let in a breeze along with thick snow flurries. "Good grief, there's almost a

foot of powder. I should've taken the snowshoes."
She sighed. "I like my steak medium rare." Then
with a wave she was gone.

Exactly the way Nash liked his steaks. Lynn
had become a pro at whipping up simple meat-
and-vegetable dishes with a baked potato on the
side for him. He always gushed over her cooking,
proclaiming it better than what was served at Delgado's. She wasn't sure if she had entirely believed
that, but it had made her feel good to hear it.

They worked well together on so many levels,
but not the most important one.

Maybe she needed to take a leap of faith and
have confidence that he would one day give her
what she needed. But if she gave him more time
and he didn't follow through, could she trust herself to walk away from him again?

It had taken all her strength to do it once before. She wasn't sure she was strong enough do
it a second time.

Lynn washed her hands and pulled out the
meat. After prepping the boneless rib eyes, liber-
ally sprinkling them with salt, she found a cast-
iron pan and put it on the stovetop to get it hot. She
washed and chopped the vegetables for a salad and
set it all in a large bowl she'd taken from the cabi-
net. After rummaging through drawers, she found
a wine corkscrew to open a bottle of Bordeaux
so it could breathe before dinner. It was a 2010

Château Branaire-Ducru. Yvonne had brought the good stuff.

She went to the window adjacent to the door and pulled back the curtain. The sun had set. Moonlight shone on the bright white snow. A pristine landscape.

Since the front of their cabin faced the other cabins a few hundred yards away, it was hard to see the hill that led to the main house and whether Yvonne was on her way back down.

In the kitchen, the oil she'd added to the pan shimmered and moved around fluidly when she tilted it, letting her know it was hot enough to get a crust on the steaks. Just as she was about to put the rib eyes on, she reconsidered. The meat would only take three minutes per side, and she didn't want the food to be cold by the time Yvonne got back.

How long did it take to run a credit card?

The west side of the cabin, where the two bedrooms were, faced the hill. From there, she'd be able to see all the way up to the back door of the lodge. She passed the first, smaller room Yvonne had claimed and went to her bedroom for a better look. Without bothering to turn on a lamp, she peeked through the curtain, hoping for a glimpse of Yvonne.

At the sight of movement headed down the hill, she smiled. "Took long enough," she said to herself.

She focused a little longer on the figure stamping through the snow as it drew closer and into the moonlight. No fuchsia coat. No slim, feminine physique.

Her scalp prickled with foreboding. It wasn't Yvonne.

Black hood pulled up over his head. Dark winter coat and pants. Fists covered in black leather gloves. Moonlight reflected off the white skull face on his ski mask.

It was *him*.

A rush of fear jetted through her veins as she stared, eyes narrowing, fingers curling at the edges of the curtain. The snowy image in front of her wavered and blurred. Her knees weakened, and she forced herself to blink, to breathe, to focus.

How did he find her? Had he followed her there?

On the ride up, it hadn't occurred to her to check the mirrors or keep an eye on the cars behind them. She hadn't imagined he would track her to the lodge.

She'd underestimated him.

Her breath tried to escape on a sob, so she clamped her lips together as she stared out the window.

He moved quickly, effortlessly through the snow down the hill.

Toward her cabin. To torture her. Rape her. Then kill her.

That's what he did to his victims.

A scream built in her chest, but she kept her mouth pinched closed. She sucked in shallow, rapid breaths through her nose, trying to think.

What was she going to do? What happened to Yvonne? Did he hurt her? Kill her?

She'd put her best friend and Earl in danger.

Oh God. He was almost there. Any minute, he'd be at the cabin.

Spinning around, she bumped into a nightstand. The lamp on top of it wobbled, but she steadied it before it fell, not wanting to make any loud noises.

She ran back to the kitchen. The pan on the stove was starting to smoke, forming a gray cloud in the room. She grabbed the phone from the hook. Pressing the receiver to her ear, she went to punch in 911 on the keypad, but there was no dial tone. Not even static. She depressed the hook switch several times.

Still, nothing.

The line was dead.

Chapter Thirteen

Pressing a hand to her temple, Lynn whispered to herself, "Think, come on, think…"

A hundred thoughts raced through her head at breakneck speed. But one stuck.

Run! Go, go!

She had to get out of there. Right now.

Pushing aside the suffocating panic, she gathered herself. She threw the phone down, the receiver knocking over the roll of paper towels onto the stove. She flew to the front door and locked it. Turning, she caught sight of the flames.

The paper towels had caught fire. If she went to the kitchen, she could put it out before it really got started. But there was no time to worry about a fire.

She raced to Yvonne's bedroom, engaged the push-lock on the doorknob and shut it from the hall. Once he got inside, he'd reach that bedroom first. If he found the door locked, he'd waste time getting in to look for her. At least she hoped so.

Then she hurried into her room. Locked that door, too. She pushed the heavy, solid oak dresser, shoving it against the door to slow him down.

Now what?

She looked around frantically. For what in particular, she didn't know. Her gaze landed on her purse. She grabbed it from the bed, unzipped it, snatched the pepper spray and stuffed it in the pocket of her jeans.

What if she hid, waiting for him to get close enough, and sprayed his eyes? Then what? Pepper spray would only slow him down. Not stop him.

Maybe she could run to another cabin and hide there. Wait until someone showed up.

But who?

She had no idea what happened to Yvonne or Earl. The landline was down. If the fire in the cabin got big enough, someone would eventually see it and come. But how long would that take? How many hours?

No one knew she was in immediate danger. She hadn't even bothered to call Nash when they'd arrived like she'd promised.

The thought of Nash was like a beacon in the darkness, guiding her. She needed to get out of the cabin and go somewhere with cell reception. But first, she had to find out what happened to Yvonne.

Lynn grabbed her phone and shoved it into her other pocket. Escaping through the front door was out of the question.

Her darting gaze settled on the window, her feet moving toward it before she had consciously made the decision. Up close she noticed the window had a triple track system. One pane on the inside, a storm window on the outside and a half screen in between.

As she unlocked the interior window, there was the unnerving slow groan of the front door.

TRK hadn't kicked it in. He must have picked the lock. Now he was inside.

Terror pulsed through her. For a precious second, she froze before hoisting the screen up out of the way and fumbling with the storm-window fastening. There was a click. She gave it a good shove, swinging the window out, and braced against the blast of frigid air.

She swung one leg over the sill and then the other, dropping to the ground below. A shock of razor-sharp cold sliced through her as her sock-covered feet sank into the snow.

If only she'd thought to grab her boots and coat before she'd bolted from the other side of the cabin.

She reached up to shut the inside window, hoping TRK would waste a little extra time searching the second bedroom as well for her, giving her an invaluable head start. She would need a big lead to get away from him. He was too fast to outrun.

The snow-covered ground was a lot lower than the floor inside had been. Her clammy fingers slipped on the bottom edge of the window as she tried to pull it closed.

To her left was an old, chunky HVAC unit. She climbed on top of it, giving her the extra height that she needed. The heavy thud of footsteps crossing the floor deeper in the cabin echoed in the bedroom. A second later the smoke detector went off, filling the air with a high-pitched beeping noise.

She slammed the interior window shut, followed by the exterior one, and didn't allow herself to hesitate, taking off up the hill.

In case he glanced out the window, looking for her, she stuck close to the tree line, where she could blend in with some concealment, and stayed off the main pathway that was bathed in moonlight.

Pumping her arms and driving her legs as fast as possible, she plowed through the drift, sinking calf-deep in the snow with every stride. She looked down, noticing her all-too-visible tracks. They might as well have been glowing in neon paint, spelling out: this way to your next victim. As soon as he ventured out to look for her, all he had to do was follow the fresh broken trail of snow.

Maybe she should have forgone the cover of the trees and used Yvonne's tracks. Too late now.

The blustery wind whipped snow around her. The cold gnawed down to her bones.

The slope of the hill, the icy gusts, the freezing snow all slowed her to a nightmarish pace. But she couldn't think about it. Dwelling on it would only impede her further.

Keep moving.

Sweat beading at her hairline, she drove her body harder, willing herself up the hill. Her feet and hands were numb with cold, but she pushed grimly toward the lodge.

She ran four miles every other day. The main house was less than four hundred yards away now. She could do this. She had to.

Snow fell in a dense curtain. One TRK would soon part.

Go, go! Faster, faster!

Her mind was spinning, her body protesting, but she kept running. With each step, she expected to hear footfalls gaining behind her, to feel hands grasping for her, or the excruciating jolt of a bullet ripping through her. But she didn't dare look back, not even a glance over her shoulder. She kept her sights locked on the lodge that was slowly—much too slowly—getting closer.

Ignoring the pain and fatigue settling in her body, she ran onward. Hard. She scrambled from the tree line and sprinted for the house, reaching out for the stair railing like a lifeline.

Her feet slid on ice as she hit the back steps of the lodge, nearly losing her balance. She dashed up the stairs to the back door. It was wide open. The screen door was the only thing partially keeping the snow out. She swung it open and hazarded a quick glance back.

TRK was nowhere in sight.

She slammed the solid door shut and engaged the dead bolt. Whirling around, she ran through the house to the front desk. She stumbled to a stop and gasped at what she saw.

Yvonne was on the floor behind the desk with her hands tied. Earl was a lump beside her, also tied. They weren't moving, but they were gagged—and tied up.

That meant they were alive. He hadn't killed them.

Lynn hurried to Yvonne and put two fingers to her carotid artery to be sure. There was a pulse. *Thank God.* She checked Earl as well and was relieved to find him still breathing.

She looked around for a knife or something to use to cut them loose, but there wasn't anything at the desk.

Hurry up! You can't stay here waiting for him to catch you.

A tear leaked from her eye at having to leave Yvonne, but she was alive. As long as Lynn stayed away from her, she'd be all right.

Lynn unzipped her friend's boots. Moving quickly, she ditched her soaked socks, trading them for Yvonne's, and then put on the warm fur-lined boots. With Yvonne's hands tied, she couldn't take her coat, but Lynn would freeze to death if she didn't find something to put on. Or somewhere warm to hide. She checked Yvonne's pockets and found the car keys.

Yes!

Knowing she didn't have a prayer of outrunning him, couldn't hope to evade him for long, she concentrated on getting to the car. It was her only chance.

She threw open the front door and hustled down the stairs of the lodge. Stumbling down the last two steps, she fell onto her hands and knees into the snow, bringing her eye level with the wheels.

Both tires were flat. She climbed to her feet and pushed around to the other side of the vehicle. The tires on the left side were also flat.

All four had been slashed to the rims.

A chilling, mind-numbing fear seeped through her. He had cut her off from any help and made sure to leave her no way to escape.

She'd have to risk going on foot. In the middle of this blizzard.

Hitting the key fob, she popped the trunk. Yvonne was always prepared for anything. There had to be something in the trunk that she could use.

Her gaze locked onto the blue-and-black winter roadside kit. She had no idea what was inside, but it had to be exactly what she needed. There was nothing else there.

Out in the elements she'd need a coat. With the kit under her arm, she rushed back inside the lodge. Lynn spotted Earl's coat on a hook behind the desk. She hurried over and grabbed the heavyweight hooded parka. Her gaze flew to the snow-shoes under the counter. Those would come in handy, allowing her to move faster, so she snagged a set and headed for the door.

A squawk of static stopped her in her tracks.

"Big Bear," a male voice said down the hall. "This is Little Bear again. Over."

A radio. There was a radio.

She dashed back through the house to where she thought the sound had come from into the living room.

"Big Bear, it's been fifteen minutes and you're still not answering. If you're in the commode, drop the newspaper and pick up. Otherwise, Mama is going to have a fit worrying."

Following the sound of the voice, she tracked the radio to a table on the far side of the wall.

She picked up the handset of the CB radio and pressed the button for the microphone. "Hello, hello."

"Who in the tarnation is this?"

"We need help up here. Call the police and the fire department," she said, and once the words left her mouth, she realized that local first responders would have no idea what they were dealing with, and it was too complicated to explain in a matter of minutes. If she had that long.

"Put my father on, Earl Epling. Right this min-ute."

"He's unconscious, but alive."

"What? Who is this?"

"I'm Lynn Delgado. If this is Ryan, you bought groceries for me and my friend Yvonne Lamber. She's unconscious, too. There isn't time for this. Please, listen to me. Contact FBI agent Nash Garner. In Laramie. Tell him that TRK followed me here. He's trying to kill me."

"Kill you? Is this some kind of sick joke?"

Holding the handset, Lynn walked around the table to the window and pulled the edge of the curtain back for a view of the hill.

Smoke wafted out of the cabin—from the bedroom window. Then she saw him. A streak of black slashing up the white hill.

He was coming. Moving to a jog.

Dread cut to her core.

"Oh God, he's coming back to the lodge," she said into the microphone. "Please, I'm begging you. Contact Special Agent Nash Garner. Laramie. My name is Lynn Delgado. Tell him I have to leave the lodge." But where was she going to go? Her thoughts careered back to the map she had perused earlier. The trails in the area had all been highlighted. One led to help. "I'm going to try to make it to the park ranger station. The tires of our car were slashed. I have to hike there. Remember, Nash Garner. If you don't contact him, TRK is going to kill me. Do you understand?"

"Yeah, okay. I'll do it."

Lynn snapped off the radio, ensuring it wouldn't

draw TRK's attention once he got back inside. Turning, she made a beeline for the main door.

By the front desk, her eye caught a glimpse of the maps. She snagged one, disrupting the pile, and rushed out through the front door. The park ranger station was less than six miles away, but she didn't want to have to rely on memory to find it in the middle of a snowstorm.

On the porch, she shoved into the coat, yanked the hood up over her head, fit her boots into the bindings of the snowshoes. Hastily, she wrenched the straps around the toe as well as the heel, tightening them. The width of the snowshoes—oversize tennis racquets—would make getting down the steps tricky.

She hit the stairs at a ninety-degree angle, taking them one at a time at a hurried pace.

At the bottom, she ran. Once she made it to the woods and onto the trailhead she needed, she no longer felt any fear. Only adrenaline and a hard-edged determination to survive. No matter what it took.

Despite how crazy it sounded in her head, she prayed for the snowstorm to worsen. Strong sustained winds and heavier snowfall. It would decrease her visibility, but his as well, making it harder for him to track her, if not impossible.

The only thing that might be able to save her was a whiteout.

Chapter Fourteen

Unable to sit still on the stool at Delgado's, Nash shifted in his seat, tapping his fingers on the bar while he waited. Never before had he felt so useless, so impotent.

Holden sat beside him, nursing a draft beer. "Just because you haven't spoken to Lynn, doesn't mean something has happened to her."

"The only cabin retreat I wasn't able to reach was the Red Tail Lodge in the Snowy Range. The call wouldn't connect. The operator said that their line wasn't operational."

"It could be down because of the storm."

True, but Nash wasn't counting on it. His mind kept circling like a buzzard around one thought. TRK might have followed her up to the retreat.

Earlier on their way from his house headed to the Turning Point clinic, Nash had been wary, ensuring they hadn't been followed, and again, after they had arrived at the clinic, he had surveilled their surroundings.

But his vigilance had faltered once he'd learned about the threatening letters and Holden had called.

If someone had been waiting at the clinic, watching Turning Point in the hopes that Lynn might show up there, and had followed them at a cautious distance to the sheriff's department, it was entirely possible that he might not have noticed. Possible that he had been too preoccupied and in a rush.

"You can't even be certain she's staying at the Red Tail," Holden said.

"I could kick myself for not asking her the name of the place." How stupid could he be? He'd told her to write it all down for him, but he could have just asked for the damn name of the lodgings. With that, he could have gotten the rest of the info on his own.

"You had a lot on your mind. It's understandable."

No, it was inexcusable.

Nash had been somewhat relieved that she would be in a remote place, out of harm's way. Now he couldn't reach her. She might be cut off, with no way to send him or anyone else a message. An easy target. Too easy.

Isolated.

Snowed in.

With no help around for miles.

He hoped to high heaven that Lynn was all right.

But something in his gut told him that she wasn't. He was going to assume the worst until he knew, without a doubt, that she was safe and sound.

There was only one way to find out.

His cell phone rang, vibrating on the polished wood in front of him. He knew who it would be and answered right away. "Tell me you can do it," Nash said without preamble.

"I've got clearance from the sheriff," Mitch said.

Relief washed through Nash, tempered by deeper worries.

"But don't get too excited just yet," Mitch continued.

"What's wrong? Spit it out."

"The snowstorm went from bad to being on steroids. It's not safe to take off in these high winds," Mitch said, and Nash clenched his jaw in frustration. "I checked with the meteorologist over at the news station. In an hour or so, the storm will start to pass. Once the winds die down to fifty-five miles per hour, we can go."

Lynn might not have that long, but he was out of options. Driving there was impossible. The Wyoming Department of Transportation had closed portions of I-80 due to the storm. WDOT wouldn't deploy crews to clear and reopen those parts of the interstate until later tonight. Wyoming Highway 130, also known as the Snowy Range Scenic Byway—a popular "cut-across" for travelers—closed annually every winter because snow lingered late and returned early at the upper elevations. To reach the lodge from Laramie left him one choice. Going by air.

"I have to warn you," Mitch said. "In order to do what you're planning the wind speed needs to be under forty miles per hour. Even at that, you HALO jumping in under these conditions is completely bonkers."

His opinion meant something. Not only had Mitch flown Black Hawks, but he had spent a couple of years as a competitive skydiver before joining the sheriff's department. He understood the risks involved better than most, but there was nowhere suitable around the lodge for Mitch to set down and land.

Once again, Nash had no better option other than strapping on a parachute and jumping.

"I'm always game for a rough, wild ride," Mitch said, "but you could get killed doing this."

"I've done dangerous jumps before."

"From a helicopter?" Mitch asked, sounding like he thought Nash was short one too many brain cells.

"No." Never. The only thing more dangerous than leaping out of a perfectly good airplane was doing so out of a helicopter, much less in the middle of a winter storm. But making sure Lynn wasn't in danger was worth any risk. "This really can't wait any longer than absolutely necessary. I have to get out there."

"Understood. I'm with you all the way. Once a brother-in-arms, always," Mitch said. "I'll run home and grab one of my parachutes and a harness for you." He lived within walking distance of the sheriff's department. In fact, his apartment was right above Delgado's.

"Thanks. What kind of chute?"

"Ram-air."

Self-inflating airfoils, known as parafoils, gave the jumper greater control of speed and direction. They also spread the stress of deployment. He couldn't ask for a better chute. "I appreciate it."

"Since we have to wait a little to take off, I suggest you get something to eat and gather everything else you'll need."

Done. After he'd called Mitch asking for the favor, Nash went home and got his gear together. "I'm at Delgado's as we speak with Holden waiting on some grub."

Before a mission, he always ate. That's what the army had taught him. Once an operation had started, it might run longer than anticipated. The last thing you wanted was to have to fight or hump out a fellow soldier on an empty stomach. If time permitted, it was best to sleep as well. It didn't matter if you weren't hungry or tired or thought yourself too nervous to eat; that was just the way it was done.

"Order me whatever you're having," Mitch said.

"Will do." He disconnected and took a heavy drink of his water. "Once the wind settles so it's safe enough to take off, we're going to head out," Nash said to Holden.

They had both agreed that it was best to let Mitch square away getting clearance without Holden present. The sheriff had already been apprised of the situation, and Nash didn't want Holden putting himself in a precarious situation, where he might look to be showing a bias because they were friends.

The sheriff was a reasonable man, the facts spoke for themselves, and Mitch was the pilot, who had to fly under less-than-desirable conditions. There was no reason for Holden to stick his neck out.

Holden patted his back with a look of relief. "You'll get out there and see that she's fine."

Nash hoped so, but he doubted things were fine.

Holden's head turned and whatever he spotted had a smile spreading across his mouth. Nash followed his gaze to Grace Clark.

She was a natural beauty. Tawny brown complexion. Long dark hair that was more curly than wavy. Petite build. But she was young. Nash guessed twenty-four, twenty-five tops. He wasn't sure how her much older brother would feel about a seven-year age gap between his little sister and Holden, and there was also the scandal to complicate matters.

But whenever his buddy laid eyes on her, he lit up like a football stadium on Super Bowl Sunday.

"Here you go," Grace said. As she went to set down a plate of cheeseburgers and fries in front of each of them, Holden took his directly from her in midair.

It was something his friend always did, but this time Nash noticed the way Holden brushed his hand against hers, like he was using any excuse to touch her.

"Thank you," Holden said. "That was quicker than expected."

"You said you were in a rush, and I aim to please." Grace flashed a dazzling smile.

"You're doing a fine job of pleasing me," Holden said. "I mean, here in the restaurant. You're great at this."

"At serving food and drinks?" she asked, her smile turning coy. "Well, thanks for the high praise."

"I'm sure you're great at plenty of other stuff, too," Holden said, and Nash shook his head, hoping his friend would do himself a favor and talk a little less. "How did you do on your final exams?"

"I aced them."

"See. I knew it. Working here full-time while earning your advanced degree and you make it seem effortless. You'll graduate with honors."

Grace smiled. "Can I get you two anything else?"

"Another order of the same," Nash said. "Mitch is coming."

"I'll go put in a third rush order. Hold the pickles and add mayo."

Holden sat up taller on the stool. "You've got an excellent memory if you remember how he takes his burger."

Grace chuckled. "You guys have been in here every night since…" Her voice trailed off as she looked at Nash, and he wasn't surprised that she was aware of the breakup. Grace cleared her throat. "With customers as frequent as you guys, any waitress-slash-bartender worth her salt would remember. I'll go put that order in." After another smile, this one shaky, less confident, she turned and left, pushing through the left swing door that led to the kitchen.

"Why do I always sound like an idiot when I talk to her?" Holden stared at the double doors like she might reappear any second.

"Why don't you just ask her out?" Nash picked up his burger and took a bite. He wasn't the least bit hungry. Worrying about Lynn had sapped his appetite, but he shoveled a few fries in his mouth, too.

"She's the sheriff's sister," Holden said, as though that explained everything.

"So?"

"So? I know what people think about me."

The scandal happened almost a year ago. The old sheriff was behind bars, right along with Holden's ex-fiancée and a corrupt judge. There was a new sheriff in town. Holden had maintained his position and his dignity. Tongues were still wagging with idle gossip, and the occasional side-eye was still being cast, but that would eventually stop.

"And?" Nash asked around the food in his mouth.

"And?"

"Please stop repeating me." Nash didn't have the patience for it tonight.

Holden took a long draw on his beer. "I can't afford to rock the boat with Daniel. He wasn't one hundred percent sure about me or my judgment, but he's given me a chance. I don't want to blow it by messing around with his sister."

"If your intentions are to mess around, then you'd certainly blow it." Nash took another bite.

"I didn't mean it like that." Holden exhaled, his shoulders sagging. "I need to be careful, is all I'm saying. Dating the sheriff's sister, my boss's sister, isn't what I'd call being *careful*."

"Seems like you're overthinking it. You don't even know if she's interested in you."

Holden scowled. "If I asked her out, you don't think she'd say yes?"

Nash wondered what it was like to be Holden, the golden boy—figuratively and literally. High school quarterback selected all-state. Chief deputy with an unblemished record. Blond hair and baby blues women fawned over. Had been next in line for sheriff. Everything came easily to him on his first time trying until that despicable scandal had cast him under a spotlight of doubt.

The sooner he put it behind him, the sooner others would also.

"Does it matter what she'd say?" Nash asked. "Apparently, you're not planning to ask her anyhow."

Holden's face twisted into an expression that made it crystal clear he was torn about what to do. Grace reemerged from the kitchen and headed to the opposite end of the bar to take someone's order. His attention again fastened to her, the look on his friend's face intensifying.

"Eat," Nash said, hoping to distract him, and gestured to Holden's untouched plate of food.

"Eat?"

He was doing it again. Nash grunted his annoyance.

"You're about to jump out of a helicopter in the middle of a winter storm. How can you stomach all that food?"

"Training." There was plenty of time for his food to digest before they'd be up in the air.

"I just wish I knew that Daniel fully trusted me," Holden said, lowering his voice. "You know?"

Not being fired and kept on as chief deputy might be as good as it was going to get. "You may have to settle for him trusting you *enough* instead of *fully*."

These things took time. Trust had to be earned, and Holden had a lot going for him. He had this way of growing on you, endearing himself to people. Before too long Holden would be in Daniel's good graces without question.

The door to Delgado's opened, letting in a gust of cold air. Daniel Clark walked in.

Speak of the devil.

Their gazes collided, and the sheriff's face tensed.

Nash set his burger down and wiped his hands on a napkin as Daniel made his way over to them. "What is it?" He hoped the sheriff hadn't changed his mind about letting Mitch fly him to the Red Tail Lodge.

Daniel took off his Stetson and clutched the cowboy hat in his hands the way a man often did when he was about to deliver bad news.

"Mitch checked with the meteorologist," Nash said. "We're going to wait until it's safe to leave. You don't have to—"

"That's not why I'm here. It turns out that Lynn left a note with Deputy Livingston that she'll be staying at the Red Tail Lodge. He was fighting with his girlfriend on the phone when Holden checked with him earlier. He was distracted and forgot. Misplaced the note. Not that there's any excuse for his oversight."

Holden rolled his eyes and shook his head while he muttered something about incompetence.

Nash couldn't deny he was irritated as well, but

Lynn hadn't forgotten to leave her contact information for him. She'd followed through.

"It's been one blunder after another with Livingston. I plan to have a stern talk with him." A grave look tightened across Daniel's face. "What jogged his memory was a call we just received from the Carbon County Sheriff's Department," Daniel said, and every muscle in Nash's body tensed. "There's been an incident at the Red Tail Lodge."

Nash's heart seemed to stop, his lungs shriveling in his chest, robbing him of oxygen.

"Lynn made it there. She contacted the owner's son on a CB radio and said that TRK had followed her up to the place. The owner and Yvonne were found unconscious and unharmed. Looks like he used chloroform on them. And," Daniel said, hesitating, "Lynn's cabin was on fire."

Nash's mind whirled, his guts twisting. His intuition that something was wrong was validated. "Was she inside?"

"No. They think the fire started before she made contact on the radio, because she told the son to call the fire department."

"How long ago did she make the call on the radio?"

Daniel's gaze fell a moment, then lifted, meeting Nash's again. "Over an hour ago, possibly longer," was the grim response.

"What?" Slamming away from the bar, Nash shoved to his feet.

"The owner's son wasn't sure how seriously he should take the things Lynn said before contacting the FBI like she asked him to. He did call the local sheriff and drove up to the lodge to see for himself first. It took them a while to make it up there on account of the storm."

Holden swore, taking the words from Nash's mouth.

Precious time was slipping away that could cost Lynn her life.

"Lynn asked the son to contact you, specifically. To let you know that she was going to try to get to the nearest park ranger station. On foot."

Things were worse than Nash feared. He scrubbed a hand through his hair. "How far away is the closest station to the lodge?"

"About six miles."

Nash squeezed his eyes shut, trying to stop the sudden roar in his ears. Time stood still. All he felt was pain. Helplessness. Utter fear for Lynn.

Six miles. In a deadly winter storm. On foot. With a serial killer chasing her.

Opening his eyes, he shut down the white noise in his ears. "She's strong. She's smart. She can make it."

Daniel nodded, though he looked doubtful. "Yeah, she will."

"And you'll be there by the time she arrives," Holden said, his voice also uncertain.

Come hell or high water, regardless of strong winds, he would be.

Chapter Fifteen

Lynn slowed to a slog. She had been switching off between jogging and walking and falling behind to plodding when each heavy, ragged breath began clawing at her lungs. The wind had been brutal, viciously lashing her with persistent gusts. Combined with the heavy snowfall, slippery conditions and diminished visibility, it was taking her forever.

She stopped entirely to rest and leaned against a tree for support. Her breath punched from her mouth in clouds. The ache in her body had deepened, sinking down to her bones. Her limbs felt leaden, and she was growing light-headed.

The first time she had taken a break, she'd rummaged through the winter roadside kit. Inside she'd found a foil blanket, gloves, packets of hand warmers—which she'd used immediately in the gloves and boots, a rope, a phone charger, a utility knife she'd put in her pocket, protein bars, a first aid kit, and a flare gun that came with yellow and red shells.

Glancing over her shoulder, she searched for a glimpse of her assailant, but all she saw were trees and a swirl of white. As if her prayer had been answered after she'd fled the lodge, the bad weather had picked up earlier. The storm had raged, visibility practically nil. She had gotten her whiteout.

For the past two hours, she had been relatively safe.

If she had been unable to see more than a few feet in front of her, then it would've been the same for him. The flip side of her circumstances was she couldn't be sure she was still going the right way with the path covered and unable to see landmarks in the distance.

Now it seemed as though the storm was passing. The wind had died down. The snow had slowed to flurries. She had no way of knowing if he had picked up her trail, and if he had, how far behind her he might be. Every few minutes she would have to check so he didn't come up on her while she was unaware.

If he did, she would be done for.

On the bright side, she should be able to figure out how far she was from the park ranger station. Lynn took out the map along with a protein bar from the emergency kit. Not having had anything to eat for hours, she was famished and fatigued. Maybe food would restore her strength.

She tore into the wrapper with her chattering teeth. Taking a few bites of the chalky peanut-butter-flavored bar, she used the dark outline of the mountains cutting through the moonlight around her to orient herself.

Medicine Bow Peak was the highest point in the

Snowy Range. The summit, at little over 12,000 feet, had only been ten miles from the trailhead she'd taken. The Laramie Mountains were to the northeast. A ridgeline she knew well, having seen it every day.

She pinpointed the Sugarloaf Park Ranger Station on the map next.

It looked as if she was going in the right direction but had veered way off the path during the whiteout. According to the map, the fastest way to get back on it was to trek down to the narrow valley that was mostly treeless. The station was less than a half mile on the other side. Based on her estimates, she had traveled at least four and a half miles, maybe five. Her body protested that she had run a marathon, and, at a minimum, she had more than a mile still to go, factoring in the added distance through the valley to get back on the trail.

Maybe she was able to get a signal here. She took out her cell phone. One bar.

She dialed Nash and waited. The call dropped. *Stupid mountains.*

It might go through to emergency services. Her cellular provider might not have coverage here, but if any other company did, they legally had to route it to a 911 call center. She tried again, dialing 911. The same result.

Lynn was tempted to scream in frustration, but

it wasn't worth if it might give away her location to the man hunting her.

Putting away her phone, she stared at the frigid landscape. The snow was making this so much harder, compounded by the higher altitude.

The valley would be at a lower elevation. From there it should be much easier, relatively speaking.

Lynn looked back again over her shoulder. No sign of him.

With any luck, she might be in the clear.

FLYING IN BAD weather was nothing new to Nash, but from inside the helicopter, with every vibration and shudder of the aircraft, he felt that today was exceptionally bad.

The weather wasn't nearly as violent as it had been a little while ago. Although he had protested, wanting to ignore the warnings about the wind, to reach Lynn that much sooner, the pilot had been wise to delay takeoff.

Mitch seemed to be using all of his concentration to keep them on course. Not to mention in the air as the potential of icing increased.

"Come on, Sienna Rose, you can do this," Mitch said.

"Are you talking to the helo?"

"Yep. I do that sometimes. Mostly when I'm worried."

"Why Sienna Rose?" Wouldn't one or the other suffice?

"Back in the army, I had a girlfriend with that double-barrel name. She was a looker and sweet on me. Told me she was saving herself for marriage. I was cool with that until I found out she had been sleeping around with everyone but me. I swore to myself that if I ever got to be the only person to pilot a particular chopper, to have her all to myself, I'd name her Sienna Rose."

That sounded like one way to work through your issues. Cheaper than hiring a therapist.

Right about now, Nash was willing to pay everything he had to take Lynn in his arms. To get the chance to make up for the all the ways he had been holding back in their relationship.

He hadn't realized that he had been. Hadn't understood that he'd been afraid.

If the last twenty-four hours had taught him anything, it was what real fear was and how the possibility of forever losing the woman he loved at the hands of TRK would devastate him. There was nothing in the world more terrifying.

The woman you love, Nash, think about it.

But there was nothing to think about. In that moment, he had never been more certain of anything in his life. He loved her.

He ran his hand over the buckles of the harness that held the attached parachute he was wearing. The revised plan was to head to the Sugarloaf Park Ranger Station. There was enough space for Mitch to land safely. From the station, Nash would head out on a snowmobile the rangers had left for him to look for Lynn, and Mitch would continue to search from the air.

Based on the flight plan, they would end up flying near the Red Tail Lodge on their way to the ranger station.

Provided things worked out, Nash wouldn't have any need to use the chute.

But he was well aware that sometimes plans were worthless while planning was always essential. Trying to get into the harness inside the helicopter would have been awkward if not time-consuming. It was easier and simpler to be prepared and discard the pack at the ranger station.

Mitch keyed his microphone that was attached on his headset. "One second, Sheriff, let me patch him in so he can hear you as well." He flipped a switch on the panel intercom, connecting Nash's headset to the radio transmission. "Go ahead," Mitch said. "He can hear you now."

"I reached out to the rangers like we discussed. They were finally able to mobilize," the sheriff said. "Unfortunately, the storm slowed them down. Two of them just headed out to conduct a search-and-rescue for Lynn."

Thank God. Additional help was on the way for her. "Good work."

"If I hear anything else," the sheriff said, "I'll let you know."

"Much appreciated."

Mitch flipped the switch on the panel back down. "Hey, look." He pointed out the windshield.

Below them there was a towering plume of smoke rising skyward from a raging fire.

Lynn's cabin.

There were other small cabins in the vicinity of the one burning. On a hilltop sat a larger main house. Flashing red and blue lights of patrol cars were out front along with a fire truck.

They had reached the Red Tail Lodge. Where a serial killer had stalked Lynn and was hunting her now.

Seeing the fire reminded him they were close, keying him up and putting him on edge.

"Do you want me to circle lower for a closer look?" Mitch asked.

Waste time on a scene that Lynn had fled? "No. The sooner we get to the ranger station, the better." Then he could get out there and search for her, too.

He looked over the topographical map again, focusing on the trailhead Lynn would have taken. But it would have been easy for her to lose her way, at night and in a snowstorm.

Gripped by emotion, he swallowed hard.

There was also no telling if that psycho had found her, gotten his hands on her. Was she alive? Injured and at the mercy of that man? Was it already too late?

Or was she still doing her best to evade that maniac?

His shoulder muscles bunched as a vast hole opened inside him. An emptiness born of the unknown. Magnified by his deepening fears.

He refused to let this get the better of him and tamped down all the negative, destructive feelings into the pit of his soul. The same way he tuned out the beep and whine of the electronics in the helicopter. If he wanted to help Lynn, he needed a cool head, laser-focused thinking, to be ice-cold with determination.

Nash chose to believe she was still breathing. He had to get to her as soon as possible.

Where there was hope, there was a chance.

TRK liked to take his time with his victims, torturing them for hours before raping and stabbing them to death. Nash needed her to survive. To stay alive, no matter what happened.

With renewed purpose, he looked back at the map.

Hang on, Lynn.

Keep moving. Keep fighting.

Hang on.

CLUTCHING THE EMERGENCY kit to her chest, Lynn finished making her way down an escarpment into the valley. Once she reached flat ground, she bent over, putting a hand on her thigh. As she caught her breath, she cursed the madness that had brought her here.

If only she had stayed out of the newspaper, she never would have captured TRK's sick interest.

It took longer than she expected to recover her breath. Lynn was beyond exhausted. Before this she would've called herself in shape. Although it was so cold that her feet and hands were numb, she was sweating buckets beneath her clothes. As much as she ached, and as tired as she was, she couldn't give up. She had to keep going until she reached help. Then she could rest, once she was safe.

Only a little farther now, and she would be at the ranger station.

She should check the time and see if she could get a signal. Her phone should work here in the valley. She fished it out from her pocket.

The screen was dark and wouldn't wake. Her phone was dead.

She should have thought to charge it earlier, but there was nothing stopping her from doing it now. Digging into the emergency kit, she found the phone charger and connected it to her cell. Zero percent flashed on the screen. Throwing both in the bag, she figured she'd give it until 15 percent. That was usually when her phone became reliable for calls.

Setting her teeth and shivering from the cold, she stood and plodded down the valley.

There were tracks in the snow. Not footprints. But those of a small vehicle. From the width and depth, she guessed a snowmobile. The tracks ran ahead of her toward the station.

That was probably where they had started. Maybe rangers were out looking for her. If they were, then it meant that Ryan had passed along her message.

Had she just missed a ranger? Had the noise of the snowmobile gotten lost in the roar of the wind? She wondered how long ago one had come through here. More importantly, how long until one came back?

Closing her eyes, she listened, but didn't pick up on the whirring motor of a nearby snowmobile. But there was the sound of something else. Far off in the distance she registered a distinct thumping beat. Perhaps a helicopter. Not close enough to see yet to be sure.

Nonetheless, she opened her eyes and looked up. The sound seemed to disappear. Had she been mistaken? Turning around, she searched the night sky. Clouds, stars and flurries. No helicopter. Then her gaze fell to the other end of the valley.

Her heart nose-dived to her stomach as *he* rounded a bend, coming into sight.

That cold-blooded killer must've assumed she would try to get to the ranger station and had probably lost his way as well in the storm. The same as her, he was using the valley to make up time.

He was relentless. A hunter.

And about a hundred yards away. Only the length of a football field separated them.

Cold, horrifying dread thrummed in her veins. *Run, run, run!*

Lynn's mind screamed at her. She whirled around and ran. The singular thought repeated in her head—a chant of survival.

One foot in front of the other, she drove herself forward, pushing to the point that she was once again, far too quickly, breathless.

And terrified.

Her lungs burning, fear cutting through every inch of her sharp as razor blades.

Glancing over her shoulder, she freaked at what she saw. He'd also had the prudence to wear snow-shoes and was running at a dead sprint, eating away at the distance between them at a startling pace.

She stumbled. Caught herself. Ran.

Beating back the panic that caused the surface threads of her sanity to unravel, she kept moving, tramping through the storm. Only she was too slow. Too tired. Even without the snow and fatigue, there was no way she could ever outrun him.

Under these conditions, his advantage was greatly amplified.

Another glance back confirmed her worst suspicions. Swinging his arms to and fro, pumping his muscular legs, his breath fogging the air, he would overtake her in a matter of minutes.

Sheer terror clawed at her. She was running out of time. It was as if a clock was ticking inside her to the rhythm of her heartbeat. The seconds of her life sliding away with each step that man took.

Keep going, she told herself over the sound of her pulse hammering in her ears.

Don't stop.

Run as fast as you can!

Adrenaline propelling her, she struggled to go faster, racing along the valley floor.

Heart in her throat, she pushed through the snow. She could see the woods and the path that led to the ranger station. But she would never make it to the path, much less the station.

Not like this.

What would Nash do? He, with his Special Forces background and FBI experience. The love of her life, who was most at home in the middle of action, on the job, instead of talking about his feelings.

Stay calm.

Use logic.

Then another voice resonated in her ears—*always think outside the box.*

The words solidified what to do. The last thing

the man chasing her would expect. The one thing her instincts warned her not to do.

She stopped running.

Unzipping the emergency kit, Lynn forced herself to stand still to keep from spilling the contents onto the ground. She fumbled around inside. Her fingers closed around the hard plastic of the flare gun.

Looking over her shoulder, she rummaged for a shell as he drew closer and closer. The crunch of his footsteps through the snow bounced off the valley walls, echoing in her ears.

Without looking down and keeping her gaze fixed on that man, she popped the shell inside the flare gun. She turned and aimed, wishing with all her heart and soul that it had been a real gun. The Ruger Nash had given her. Loaded with bullets.

Because for the first time in her life, she wanted to kill someone—that man.

Then she squeezed the trigger, the gun bucking in her hand.

A deafening crack resounded through the valley, making her assailant freeze. Only fifty yards from her. Mere seconds of hesitation before he resumed charging toward her.

Damn it! It must've been the yellow shell. A blank, delivering a loud gunshot-like sound to scare off bears.

She looked in the bag. There were four red

shells. Fifty yards shrank to forty. She fished out a red one. Dumped the used cartridge and reloaded.

He was thirty yards away.

She aimed.

Fired.

Once more she felt the recoil. The flare streaked straight ahead and hit him. He stumbled back, his arms flailing as the flare blazed, burning dead center. With the protective layer of his coat, she had no idea if it would burn through his clothes to cause any real damage.

But with him distracted and focused on something other than her, she started running.

Lynn reloaded another red shell while keeping her feet moving. She looked back to take aim. This time at his head, where she knew it would hurt, if not kill him.

He was throwing snow on his chest, causing the flare to sputter out quickly.

As she squeezed the trigger, his gaze lifted.

The flare hissed forward. But this time he dived, facedown into the snow, and it missed.

Lynn took off again.

The air was so crisp it was brittle. Her lungs were on fire, her legs aching with each jarring step. It was surreal, as though they were the only two people in the world. A gasping, exhausted woman unable to move fast enough and an unrelenting murderer steadily closing the gap between them.

She couldn't let him catch her. She had to find a way to save herself.

In the kit, she snagged another shell. Trying to reload and hold on to the bag at the same time, her feet faltered. Her knees began to buckle, and the cartridge slipped from her fingers into the snow.

Reaching out for a tree, she righted herself.

She couldn't afford to go back for the shell. All she could do was keep moving, even though she had nowhere to go. Nowhere to hide.

Don't think about it! Keep. Going. She was breathing hard, frosty air scorching her throat. If only there was a way to call for help. But the phone wasn't charged and even if it was, how would help get there in time? She was all alone.

No one in sight. Only that man. Only her own ragged breathing, and his, making a sound.

She hazarded another quick glance behind her.

God, he was so close. Less than fifteen yards. Maybe ten. The crunch of snow behind her bit her ears.

One last red cartridge left in the kit. Gasping, her heart threatening to burst, she slowed despite her mind protesting. Unable to keep hold of everything, she grabbed the shell and dropped the bag. Reloaded. Whirled to shoot.

He was right up on her. He lunged, thrusting his body through the air, and tackled her to the ground.

She hit the valley floor hard with him on top of her. He wrenched her hand holding the gun up. Her finger squeezed. The last flare—her last chance—streaked up into the air.

Chapter Sixteen

"Did you see that?" Nash asked, pointing out the windshield.

A flare shot up, cutting through the dark sky.

"Yeah, I did. Hard to miss. I'll circle around to where it came from." Mitch pulled on the cyclic control stick, turning into the wind, taking them east.

Toward the valley.

"Can you get lower?" Nash asked. With the darkness, it was hard to see from the air despite the full moon and its light shining off the snow.

"I'll do my best." Mitch flew over countryside, getting so low that the tips of the trees scraped the underbelly of the helo. "Sorry about that, Sienna Rose. I can do better." He adjusted a bit, taking them slightly higher. Once they reached the valley, he dipped lower but stayed above it. "It's too narrow to fly through it."

That wasn't what Nash wanted to hear, but he said, "Understood."

The flare had been a signal from Lynn. In his gut, he knew it. What were the odds of someone else wandering around in this area, in a blizzard, shooting flares?

His guess was zilch.

A glistening swath of white, sprinkled with

trees, ran west to east. At the western end, it was wide, but narrowed the farther east it ran. On the map, the valley looked like a dagger. Not far from the eastern point was the ranger station.

There!

Beyond a cluster of trees were two individuals, both in dark clothing, wrestling on the icy, snow-covered ground.

"It's Lynn," he said, half to himself and partly to Mitch.

"We could head to the ranger station. Drop you in. From there, you could backtrack on a snow-mobile," Mitch said, but Lynn was literally fighting for her life and didn't have that kind of time. "The wind is still high. It would be safer for you."

"But not for her. Get us to the minimum altitude for me to deploy a chute."

"I'll take us to two thousand feet AGL," Mitch said, referring to *above ground level*.

"Make it one."

Mitch grimaced. "That's madness. Two is pushing it."

"You know we can do it lower."

"The lowest recorded altitude for someone to open a chute at terminal velocity and survive is eight hundred feet. Even extreme athletes don't go that low."

"I'm not asking for eight hundred. I'm telling you a thousand." Nash glared to convey his seriousness. They did not have time to squabble about his safety. Get him the altitude and he'd get to Lynn. "Do it," he snapped.

"It's your funeral," Mitch said.

Better his than Lynn's. But he wasn't going to die on this jump, because he needed to survive long enough to save her.

Mitch complied, taking them to one thousand feet AGL. "All right. I'll try to hold her steady."

Nash unbuckled his seat belt, removed his headset and got into position at the door.

"I'll have the sheriff contact the rangers," Mitch said, "and I'll keep the light on Lynn."

Nodding his thanks, Nash opened the door. He waited for Mitch to steady the helo as much as he could, and then he jumped.

LYNN'S ASSAILANT YELLED obscenities at her. "First, you run, making me chase you and take care of this in the snow when we could've done it back at the cabin." He was furious. His eyes burned hellfire, and she felt the same as she struggled against him. "Now you want to shoot me with a flare." He smacked her with the back of his fist.

Pain exploded in her face. Her vision swam along with her brain.

"I was going to make it quick," he said. "Instead, I'm going to have some fun."

A helicopter cut overhead, a spotlight washing over them and then moving away, putting them back in the darkness.

The man looked up at the sky.

The chopper stayed close, possibly hovering nearby. She couldn't be certain because her focus wasn't on the helicopter. Or her attacker, who had taken a position on top of her.

She concentrated on the utility knife in her pocket as she gripped it.

Slipping it from her coat pocket, she unfolded it with one hand and it made a slight click.

He glanced down at her, their eyes meeting.

Without hesitation, she jammed the blade into his thigh.

He roared back in pain, and she didn't give that sick SOB a chance to recover, to retaliate.

She rammed her knee up between his legs. When he doubled over, bringing his face closer, she slammed the heel of her palm up into the bridge of his nose.

The impact pushed him far enough back, freeing her hips. And her legs. She kicked him once, her bootheel connecting with his stomach. Twice. The thrust landed in his chest, shoving him farther back.

Lynn flopped onto her stomach and scrambled away. She spotted a dark figure floating from the sky. Parachuting down.

Nash.

It had to be him.

He was almost to the valley floor. But he wasn't close enough to help her.

A whisper of gunshots echoed off the valley

walls. She glanced over her shoulder. Her attacker had drawn a gun, silencer attached.

Ping! Ping! A chilling sound that scraped along her nerve endings as bullets struck the helicopter, forcing it to veer off and ascend. The spotlight danced around, not staying focused on any one thing while the chopper zigged and zagged, climbing higher.

The man lowered his gun, redirecting his aim.

Four more muffled pops of gunfire. She turned back to see holes puncturing Nash's parachute. His body jerking as though he'd also been hit. The material of the chute fluttered and crumpled, and he plummeted in free fall.

No! Please, please, no!

BULLETS RIPPED THROUGH the canopy above Nash's head. Parafoils burst with a loud pop-pop-pop. Another bullet struck his Kevlar vest. But the last tore through his arm, shredding muscle. Adrenaline pumping inside him right along with the pain. Refusing to focus on the latter, he let the former fuel him as he braced for what was to come next.

The chute deflated, sending him into a rapid descent. Dread fisted a tight knot in his stomach. In a desperate act, he grasped the chute lines, knowing it wouldn't slow his fall.

There was nothing he could do but steel himself for an ugly impact.

He glimpsed Lynn—staring at him, face contorted in horror. Then he saw that bastard going for her again.

A blind rage consumed him, burning inside him like a piece of hot metal right before he struck the ground a lot harder and faster than he'd hoped. A gust of wind snatched the chute as he tucked into a roll, the way his training had taught him. But the wind dragged the chute across the ground, hauling him with it until he smashed into the side of a tree, his head slamming against the solid bark.

LYNN'S INSIDES TWISTED harder than ever before watching Nash get shot and crash to the ground. Then he had been slammed into a tree. On impact she heard a crack.

She thought she might puke.

He couldn't die. Not like this. Not because of her.

The helicopter changed position, staying high and casting the spotlight on her. She kept moving, crawling forward through the light, trying to will her legs to stand. To run to Nash. To help him. He wasn't moving.

A big hand locked onto her ankle. Then there was a yank on her leg. *Oh no!* He had her. Why wouldn't he just let her go? Another brutal tug and she was wrenched backward through the snow.

Screaming and clawing at the icy ground, she thrashed, struggling to hold on to something. Bitter cold snow slipped through her hands.

He fired the weapon near her head but into the ground. She froze and shuddered. Trying to outrun him was one thing. Trying to outrun a bullet was impossible.

Still, she refused to give in.

Desperation flared hot under her skin. She shoved her hand into her jeans pocket for the only weapon she had left.

Something sharp bit into her calf. She shrieked in agony. A blade twisted in her flesh, and she could no longer crawl, could no longer run. Groaning through the fog of pain, she pried the pepper spray from her pocket.

He pulled the knife out of her leg and flipped her over as though she was a fish he intended to gut. Grabbing hold of the edge of her coat, he dragged her beneath him, locking her legs with his hips.

Holding the blade, he stabbed down at her. She raised her left arm, blocking him. The knife tore at the coat, down to her arm, drawing blood and searing pain. He kept slashing at her, cutting her shoulder. Her cheek. Intent on killing her. Slicing her to pieces.

Any second, he'd slit her throat.

Determinedly, closing her eyes, holding her breath, she lifted the pepper spray and depressed the release button.

He howled in anger, rearing off her. Dropping on all fours, he rubbed snow in his eyes. She wormed away from him on her back. Fearful that if she took her gaze from him that he would attack her again like some horror movie villain.

Footfalls crunched across the snow behind her.

The man brushed the snow from his face and turned in her direction. Lifted his weapon. But not at her. His aim was higher.

Her heart seized, eyes closing reflexively as a gunshot rang out.

She stilled and realized the sound had been different. Louder. No sound suppressor. Peeling her eyes open, she dared to look. The man had been thrown onto his back from the impact of the bullet.

Nash stormed past her with a slight limp, heading for her attacker, weapon at the ready. He was all right.

She didn't know how that was possible. There was no way any ordinary man could have survived something like that and keep on fighting. But Nash Garner was anything but ordinary.

He was too damn tough and stubborn to die without meeting his objective.

The spotlight from the helicopter followed Nash, bathing his movements in light. Her attacker sat up, also fighting until the end, and raised his gun.

Two more shots fired. Again, like thunderclaps, too loud to have come from a suppressor. The man's gun skittered from his hand, and he squirmed in pain. Wounded, but he was alive.

Nash punched him and tossed him onto his

stomach. He threw a knee into her assailant's back and handcuffed his hands behind him. Then Nash put zip ties around his ankles.

Lynn gathered herself, sitting upright, clutching her wounded arm.

Holstering his weapon, Nash ran to her. He knelt in the snow, bringing her into his arms.

Tears prickled her eyes as she burrowed her face into his chest. She clung to him, astonished that he was there. Grateful that he'd found her in time.

The sound of snowmobiles rose above the thump-thump of the helicopter. Rangers were closing in.

"It's over. We've got him," Nash said. He kissed the top of her head, holding her tight. "Are you okay?" His voice was heavy with emotion. He touched her arm gingerly and tried to pull back to look at it, but she kept holding on to him, unable to let go.

She opened her mouth to answer him but all that came out was a sob that was a mix of joy and relief.

"Shh." He stroked her hair. "I've got you, and I'm not going anywhere."

The nightmare was over.

They were both alive.

She was in Nash's arms.

Nothing else mattered.

Chapter Seventeen

A heavy cloud of darkness lifted.

Lynn opened her eyes. The world blurred. Then ceiling tiles with tiny holes came into focus. White walls. Dim fluorescent lights. Antiseptic smell. The faint sound of a machine beeping. An IV in her arm. Hospital bed.

Slowly, it came back to her. Helicopter ride back to Laramie. The surgery for her calf. Tendons had been severed when she was stabbed.

Memories ricocheted in her mind. Running for her life. *Him* catching her. The exhaustion. The blinding pain. Though she felt little now thanks to the drugs pumping in her system.

He had cut her so many times. Would have killed her, too.

If not for Nash.

She swallowed against the dryness in her throat. The stitches in her cheek pulled at her skin. There were more on her shoulder and arm.

A toilet flushed nearby. She turned her head toward the closed bathroom door in her room. Water ran. The faucet shut off.

The door opened. Nash came out, meeting her gaze. Intense gray eyes locked onto her. The smile that spread across his mouth tugged at her heart. All she wanted to do was kiss him.

"You're awake." He came to her side, sat on the edge of the bed and took her hand in his.

"I thought you left. Went home."

"I cleaned up while you were in surgery. But I was back long before it was over."

Tightening her fingers around his, she looked him over. He'd showered and changed. Now he wore a black T-shirt. There was a bandage around his left biceps.

"What happened to you?"

"No big deal. Took a bullet. Got a concussion," he said casually, like it could be remedied with a Band-Aid and aspirin.

She doubted that there was anything that could bring him down. Still, he was human.

Lynn grimaced. "Are you going to be okay?"

"It's nothing for you to worry about."

"If you're hurt, then I'm worried."

A faint smile pulled at his lips. "I've survived worse. No permanent damage. I'll have to do some physical therapy. But so will you."

She moved her injured leg. A slight ache coursed through the wound. Once the drugs wore off it would be a different story. "Maybe we can do it together." She stopped short of saying *as a couple*.

Dr. Lewis came into the room. "Nice to see you awake, Ms. Delgado. The surgery went well. You'll have to use a cane for a few days and you'll have a bit of a limp for a couple of weeks. Then after some physical therapy, it'll be like it never happened. Aside from a small scar."

Glancing at Nash, Lynn wondered if she'd ever be able to forget what happened. He must have read the look on her face.

"You're going to heal," he said, "and you're going to move on from this. I promise."

She swallowed the emotion rising in her throat and nodded because she believed him.

"You have your share of cuts, bruises and abrasions," the doctor said, "But he's right. You'll heal. We ran an IV drip for you because you were also dehydrated. We'd like to keep you overnight. You've been through a very traumatic experience."

"No, I want to go home." She tried to sit up and winced from the protestation of her body. Exhaustion forced her back down to the bed, her head throbbing.

"She'll stay the night," Nash said to the doctor.

"I'd rather be with you."

Never had she thought of herself as someone who would *need* another person. She had spent so many years being independent, never clinging. Yet here she found herself hating the thought of being separated from him. Tonight, she needed him.

"You will be." A grin tipped up the corner of his mouth. His thumb stroked the pulse point in her wrist. Slow, soothing circles. "I'm not going anywhere."

The way he spoke the words flooded her heart with warmth.

"Now that we have that settled," Dr. Lewis said, "I'll let you get some much-needed rest. We can discharge you in the morning."

She nodded. "Thank you."

The doctor left, shutting the door. Nash got up and drew the curtain around the bed, giving them more privacy.

Turning to him as he sat back down, she asked, "How are Yvonne and Earl Epling?" Guilt and remorse coursed through her over endangering them.

"They're both okay other than headaches. TRK used chloroform on them. Mitch will fly back out tomorrow, pick Yvonne up and take her home, where she can recuperate from the ordeal."

"What about her car?"

"We'll figure it out," Nash said. "Easy enough to get tires replaced and have someone drive it over. She knows you're okay and that I'm not leaving your side."

"I feel so bad about everything." She thought about the fire she'd accidentally started. "It's my fault the cabin burned down."

He kissed the back of her hand. "That's what insurance is for. It'll cover the damages." His voice was so soft, reassuring. Deep and so sexy. "You have nothing to feel bad about." He took off his boots. "Scoot over."

She made room for him in the bed and he lay down beside her, wrapping his uninjured arm around her shoulder, bringing her body to rest against his.

This was the best place in the world. In his arms.

Lynn put her head on his chest. "What's going to happen to TRK? And who is he?"

"They patched up his gunshot wounds. I didn't hit anything vital. He's on a different floor. His wrists and ankles are handcuffed to the bed. He's not going anywhere. The Laramie police chief volunteered two of her officers to guard him for the rest of the night when she heard what was happening. The sheriff was happy to accept her offer since his deputies haven't slept. They have instructions not to underestimate that man or lower their guard. We'll transport him to the sheriff's office tomorrow and interrogate him there. So far, no word on his identity, and he's not talking. At least not yet."

She'd been through so much. They'd been through so much, together, to get here. "Are you always like *this* on the job?"

"What do you mean?"

"The way you were out there in the valley." Unstoppable. Unrelenting. Unbelievable. "You really went above and beyond to get a serial killer."

He eased onto his side, so they were face-to-face, and looked down at her, staring into her eyes.

"Everything I did was for you." Cupping her face, he caressed her jaw with his thumb, and she loved the feel of his calluses on her skin. "I'll always fight like hell for you, Lynn."

The shadows under his eyes. The injuries he had sustained. Jumping out of a helicopter in a storm...for her. The way he was looking at her right now, with such warmth and passion and tenderness. It all coalesced, making her wonder if there might be a real chance for them.

"I was wrong for thinking that you had a propensity for violence," she said in a whisper, ashamed of herself. "That you could ever hurt a suspect deliberately. You could have beaten TRK, could've killed him."

"Believe me, I was tempted."

"But you didn't. You showed far more self-control than I would have in your shoes. I'm sorry I doubted you."

"How can I blame you? I never showed you that side of myself. Never let you into my world. Never explained anything."

"I understand that you're not used to opening up." Ignoring every hard question and putting her doubts on the back burner. She was aware he'd worked with black ops units as a ranger doing highly classified stuff. Volunteered for joint terrorism task forces with the FBI. Things that required him to be secretive. Hardened. She knew that a certain sort—an alpha, lone wolf, protector—was well-suited for that type of work. "But I need you to confide in me. Not all at once. When you're ready."

"The truth is I have kept you at a distance when you wanted to get closer because… I was afraid."

Her heart stammered. Nash Garner afraid? "Of what?"

"Rejection," he said, and the air caught in her throat. "That you'd see me as damaged. Something to fix. Not someone you could love."

He wasn't Humpty Dumpty. He was a man, with flaws, like everyone else. Her job wasn't about fixing people, it was about helping them, but he wasn't a client.

Nash was the man she already loved.

She pulled back. Not entirely, just enough to see him better. "You're so good at listening," she said, putting her hand on his chest. "At asking me the right questions. At making me feel seen. Like you truly know me. That's all I want to do for you in return. For you to know that you have a safe space with me. I promise you that I will never seek to fix you."

Some of the unease left his face. "I don't talk about my past because it sucked. It wasn't happy like yours." He covered her hand that was pressed to his chest with his own. "My mom died when I was really young. My father was a good man. But a hard man. Strict. He ended up having a heart attack."

"How old were you?"

"Twelve. Too old, too far past the peak of cuteness, with too much of a nervous stutter for people to consider for adoption. Unlike my brothers, who found stable families that wanted them. Unfortunately, not together."

She knew that he was the eldest. That there were six years between him and the twins.

"I felt guilty for a long time over not being able to keep us together," he said.

"It wasn't your fault. You were a child."

"Still. The reason I joined the army was to have a solid job with health benefits so I could be their guardian, but by then it was too late. They had adjusted and were happy."

The weight of it was visible in his eyes, the sudden strained tension in his shoulders. He had never let it go. She couldn't begin to imagine what it must've been like for him, or his brothers. Twins, separated and raised by different families.

"How was the foster care system for you?" It was a toss of the dice. Some kids found nurturing placements. Others didn't fare so well.

His jaw clenched. He was silent for a moment, as if gathering his thoughts. "What do you want to know?" His tone sharpened. "About the beatings at some homes? How they made sure not to leave bruises?" The strain of their discussion was evident on his face. "About the state facilities that were like prisons where I had to fight other kids for food, for a warm blanket? Fight to make sure I wasn't the one getting injured?"

Her heart bled for him. She was furious at the system and sick for him. "Why didn't you tell me?" She had asked about his childhood so many times, fished around for stories, and had only been given clues, fragments of information. Not enough to form a complete picture.

"Because it's hard." His gaze fell from hers. "I packed it all away with everything else painful. It's better to move on. Leave that stuff in the past."

"Oh, Nash."

"See, that's exactly what I don't want." Tension pulled at his mouth. "You feeling sorry for me. It made me strong. Tough. It drove me to the army. Where I found a different kind of family."

He was a survivor. Nash had made it through the unspeakable loss of both parents at a young age, the foster care system, violence, psychological trauma.

"I want you to trust me the way you trusted your army unit." It wasn't a direct correlation, but the understanding that gleamed in his eyes told her it was a relevant one that struck a chord. "I admire your strength," she said. "That's what saved me. That's what was needed, your drive, your intestinal fortitude, to capture that man who was hell-bent on killing me."

The world could be a scary place. As she recently learned, much more frightening than she ever imagined. Men like Nash leveled the playing field, giving those demons, like TRK, something bigger and mightier to be afraid of.

"I don't talk about my work because it takes me to a dark place," he said. "My job requires me to shut down my emotions, but not my conscience. When I'm with you, I'm happy, and that's what I want to focus on. Not replaying the worst parts of my day. The ugly, horrible things that I've seen." Pain crossed his face. "If I could change for you, be the man that you want, that you deserve, I would." He let out a haggard breath.

"Don't say such a thing. I never wanted you to change. Only to share. I'm lucky to have you. *All* of you. Because you are *not* broken." He was beautiful. Perfect just as he was. "You're amazing. The most spectacular and hottest man I've ever seen."

The tension in him lifted. He rubbed his thumb over her bottom lip, making her pulse quiver right along with her thighs. "You give me a reason to look forward to the future. I want everything with you. House. Kids. All of it. I never had that desire before I met you. Lynn…" His caress dipped to her chin and ran along her throat, sending a shiver of pleasure through her. "Lola, I love you."

Her heart squeezed at those precious words she'd always hoped to hear. He was the kind of man who would never say such a thing unless he meant it. Tears of joy welled in her eyes. "I never stopped loving you from the moment I first admitted it."

Lowering his head, he brushed his lips over hers. A rush of hot desire ran through her veins, melting her against him.

And they were back in their bubble. That sacred place where nothing else existed. Nothing else mattered other than being together.

She surrendered to his kiss as his arms came around her, holding her so close until the beat of his heart thrummed through her chest, falling in sync with her own.

No longer wrestling her feelings, she opened to him. She breathed easier, sinking against him, but kissed him harder, letting her hunger for him slide into every stroke of her tongue over his.

Desire flared white-hot, his touch fanning the flames. She lost herself in him, in the strength of his body, in the harsh moan that rumbled up his throat.

This was everything she had wanted. His vulnerability. His warmth.

His love.

For him to be all hers.

Doubt still lingered. She hoped this wasn't a case of onetime sharing. It might be all too easy for him to put up a wall between them again come tomorrow. She couldn't go back to that no matter how much she loved him. They had to be able to grow together for this to work. Only time would tell.

With a groan, he broke the kiss. "If we don't stop, one of us might bust stitches." His body pressed against the length of hers, and she could feel he wanted her as desperately as she wanted him. "Possibly both of us."

She ran her hand down the ridges and valleys of the muscles in his torso and unbuckled his belt. "I'm willing to risk it if you are. Besides, we're in a hospital. They can easily replace them."

"I know I haven't always shown the most restraint in the bedroom where you're concerned." He kissed her again before drawing his mouth away with a tender smile. "I can wait. Until we're out of here and you're feeling better."

How admirable.

She drew down his zipper. "But I can't."

Chapter Eighteen

In the observation room that had one-way glass overlooking the adjacent interrogation room, Nash grabbed a chair for Lynn. "Sit."

"I'm fine," she said, holding on to a cane for support.

"Sit," he said, this time more firmly, and she compiled. Nash turned to Holden. "I'm surprised you're here for this. I thought you'd be knocking down the Crombies' door."

Holden sighed. "Don't get me started. The judge said since I told him I wouldn't need the warrant and he didn't have anything on the docket this morning that he wasn't coming in until this afternoon."

"Do you want me to give him a call?" the sheriff asked. "See what I can do?"

"No, sir." Holden shook his head. "I made my bed. Now I've got to lie in it. I'll have the warrant later today."

The door to the interrogation room opened. The two officers from the Laramie Police Department hauled in Lynn's assailant. He wore chains between the cuffs on his wrists and ankles. Jangling into the room, he took short steps to the chair and plopped down. The officers attached the chain to the bar on the table that was bolted to the floor. He leaned forward, bringing his head to his hands, and brushed his reddish-brown hair from his face,

Lynn gasped. "I know him."

"You do?" the sheriff asked.

"No, I mean I've seen him before."

"At the Silver Springs center," Nash said. "The last time you went to visit your aunt Miriam. I didn't get a chance to tell you. There's video footage of him marking your vehicle right before he spoke to you."

Nash looked over the man. He was doing a good job of hiding his discomfort from the bullet wounds in his shoulder, forearm and thigh. The hospital had been instructed not to give him any pain meds this morning.

"Yes, I remember," she said slowly, nodding. "He told me he was considering the facility for his mother and asked me what I thought of the place. He was so nice. Charming. Even funny."

"Are you sure you're up for watching the interrogation?" Nash asked her.

"I can't bury my head in the sand. I need to be a part of this process, not lying at home in bed watching television. It's important."

He agreed. This would help her heal faster, but he didn't want to push her to do something she wasn't ready for.

"Are you sure you're not too close to this to handle the interrogation?" Daniel asked. "Agent Hammond is one phone call away."

"No, I've got it." Nash wanted to throttle that man until he was no longer breathing but he would never let emotion interfere with his job.

"This might be personal for him," Lynn said, her voice confident and strong, "but he's capable of being a consummate professional."

Nash put a hand of thanks on her shoulder. It was nice having her fully in his corner. Having a partner who knew the darkest things about him and believed in him nonetheless.

"Okay." The sheriff nodded. "I had to ask."

The two officers left the interrogation room. After a knock on the observation door, one stuck his head inside. "We're going to take off now, Sheriff, unless you need something else from us."

"No, we're good. Thank you. Tell Chief Nelson I appreciate the assistance."

"Sure. No problem." The officer nodded and left.

"I owe her a phone call to tell her myself," Daniel said. "I'm still surprised she helped. She's been so brusque with me since I took over."

"It's not you," Holden said. "It's her. She's got a bit of a chip on her shoulder."

"You wouldn't say that about her if she was a man in a difficult leadership position," Lynn pointed out.

Holden conceded with a one-shoulder shrug.

"Whatever the reason for the assistance," Daniel said, "I want to keep the good will flowing between our departments."

Nash gave Lynn's shoulder a little squeeze, and she responded with a supportive smile. Then he went into the tiny interrogation room. Meeting the man's dark brown eyes, he unbuttoned his suit jacket and took the chair opposite him at the small, battered table.

"Special agent Nash Garner," the man said. "I'm surprised they're letting you conduct this interview. Considering the conflict of interest."

Nash swallowed, taken aback. This was the first time he'd started an interrogation feeling as though he was out of his depth. How did he know his name? How did he know there was a conflict of interest because of Lynn?

Keeping his features bland, Nash refused to be thrown off-kilter.

Maybe one of the officers had mentioned Nash's name. It was possible the implied conflict was regarding the fact that Nash had been the one to shoot him.

"Would you like a cup of coffee before we begin?" Nash offered.

"No."

"You've been read your rights," Nash said, to make it clear on playback of the recording of the interrogation. "Do you understand the charges?"

"I do." He was calm and collected for a man

facing three counts of murder and one count attempted.

It was disturbing.

"Cooperating now will only help you later." Any moment, he could invoke his right to have a lawyer and clam up. That was the last thing they wanted. Regardless, he had to ask the question. "Do you want your attorney present during this interview?"

"No."

Again, unsettling. "Please state your name for the record," Nash said.

They still didn't know who this guy was. No identification had been found on him. The DNA search had failed to turn up a match. At this point, they were running his picture against DMV records.

"There's one problem," the guy said, "with the charges."

"And what's that?"

"I'm not TRK. I didn't kill anyone. In Colorado," he said, adding the last two words after a slight pause, his eyes narrowing, a devious smile playing at the corner of his mouth.

"We have video footage of you marking Lynn Delgado's car with TRK's calling card."

"Because I did," he said, lightly.

"Yet you're claiming *not* to be TRK?"

"Correct," he said, and Nash wondered what

game this guy was playing. "Before this day is over, you're going to come to realize two things."

"Enlighten me. What are they?"

"I wasn't in Colorado when those women were murdered. I was three states away for one of them and out of the country when the last one was killed."

"Great," Nash said incredulously. "Then giving us your name will help us to corroborate that sooner."

"Which brings me to the second thing. You and I are the same."

Nash sat back in his chair ramrod straight. "We are nothing alike."

"We'll see if your response changes by the end of the day."

"What's next?" Nash let his voice sound amused. "Are you going to deny trying to kill Ms. Delgado?"

"Nope."

Narrowing his eyes in suspicion, Nash didn't like this.

"But here's the thing," the guy said, "she seems like a nice woman. I didn't want to hurt her."

Okay. He was going to go with the insanity defense. Voices told him to do it. He had no control over stalking and stabbing her. "So you admit to trying to kill her?" Nash asked.

"Sure. Why not? You've got me red-handed on that one."

Nash should have been jumping for joy that the

guy had confessed, on the record, but instead his gut was churning with warning.

"This is the part where I ask for a lawyer," he said, rattling his chains.

"You're a little late. Should have asked for one before you confessed."

"Oh, no, you misunderstand." The guy laughed. Had the audacity to laugh like this was all one big joke. "The lawyer isn't for me. It's for you and the sheriff." He gestured at the one-way glass with his chin. "I want the district attorney involved."

"The DA already is. She filed the formal charges." Or at least she would later today.

"This time she's needed to authorize my immunity deal."

Now Nash was the one laughing, though there wasn't anything funny about the situation. "You've given us a confession. You're not getting immunity."

The guy placed both palms down on the table. His hands were rock steady. Then he gave a long exhale as if he was bored. "You never asked me *why* I tried to kill her."

Nash's gut twisted into a greasy knot of tension, but he kept his gaze cool and hard. "All right, I'll play along. Why did you do it?"

"Because I was hired to."

If Lynn hadn't been sitting, she would've keeled over from the shock.

At first, she wanted to reject what she had heard. Call the man a liar.

"Hired by who?" Nash asked.

A wicked smile spread across the man's lips. "I couldn't simply kill her," he said, avoiding the question. "It had to be done in a way that would never point back to the person who wants her dead. It was my clever idea to make it look like TRK. Complicated things, though, because TRK stabbed his victims. Do you know how many times I could've shot her and been done with it?"

Lynn recalled with horrifying clarity how in the valley he had shot at the snow to make her stop moving when he could have easily put a bullet in her. And he had also said something about intending to make it quick.

This was really happening.

It wasn't over.

"You need a name," said the man chained to the table in the other room. "Right? Without it, how do you keep Lynn Delgado safe? How do you stop the person who paid me from hiring a replacement to finish the job?"

The thought hadn't occurred to her. That someone else might be sent to kill her.

Her mind was reeling. Who wanted her dead so badly that they would hire a contract killer?

Both Holden and the sheriff glanced at her with concern before turning their attention back to the interrogation room.

"To get what you need," that vile man said, "you've got to give me what I need. Immunity from all crimes I've committed. Feel free to throw in a clause excluding any crimes related to the real TRK since I'm not him, okay, my friend."

Nash jumped to his feet, his chair scraping back against the floor. "I'm not your friend."

"Figure of speech, but it doesn't change the fact that we're the same."

Nash clenched a hand into a fist. "We can't give immunity to a ghost. What's your name?"

Lynn looked between the sheriff and Holden. "Is he really going to get that monster immunity? Let him get away with everything he's done?" That was so unlike Nash.

The sheriff raised a palm, signaling her to hold on a minute.

The guy shook his head. "No name until the DA is here and prepared to agree to the deal."

"Why are you stalling?" Nash asked.

"Let's just say it's in the interest of self-preservation. The DA might choose to hem and haw for a few days, mulling things over. For Ms. Delgado's sake, I would advise against that. But as for me, you can't move me until you know my name. Once I'm transferred to the county detention center, I'm as good as dead."

"Why?"

"They'll make sure I can't talk."

They?

"You have proof of the contract?" Nash asked.

"Irrefutable. I'll get off as a result of the deal but the person responsible, the one who hired me, won't."

Nash stalked to the door and grabbed the knob.

"Hey, buddy," the guy said, causing Nash to hesitate, and she could practically feel his burning irritation. "Can I get that coffee now while I wait? Black is fine."

Slamming the door behind him, Nash left and entered the observation room.

Using her cane for support, Lynn stood and faced him. She was surprised how fragile her legs felt, like thin glass that could be shattered with the careless brush of a hand. "You can't seriously be considering this. Are you?"

Taking a breath, Nash grasped both her shoulders. His grip firm yet loving. "This is not a game we can win. I knew something was off the minute he opened his mouth. I wasn't in charge in there. He was. Because he's holding all the cards."

"He watched me for days. Held me at gunpoint. Stalked me. Stabbed me. Tried to kill me and you." The distress flooding his face silenced her.

"I'm painfully aware. But we need his cooperation to learn who is behind this. He'll only give it in exchange for immunity."

"There has to be another way." She wanted justice. To hell with that, she wanted vengeance. On the person who was behind this and on the contract killer.

"It has to be Todd Burk," Holden said. "The Iron Warriors have that kind of money from the drugs they traffic and the resources to do this."

"Allegedly," the sheriff said. "As far as I know, this department has never been able to prove anything."

"They have guys sitting in county lockup as we speak," Holden said, "capable of silencing that man. I'm telling you it has to be them. He said *they.*"

"Sometimes your instincts seem to be right on the money," the sheriff said. "And sometimes they're way off base. From the old reports I read, any time someone from the Iron Warriors is brought in for questioning, instead of talking, they lawyer up."

Holden straightened. "We can't be afraid to pursue this."

The sheriff put his hands on his hips. "I'm not afraid to do my job. I just don't see the point of prematurely riling a hornet's nest."

Nash stepped between them, throwing Holden a look that Lynn couldn't read. Whatever it conveyed, Holden backed down and backpedaled.

"You're the sheriff," Holden said. "Not me. You're right. We need evidence, not me jumping to conclusions. I'm going to go check and see if there's been any progress with ID'ing that fellow." He excused himself from the room.

"Does Todd Burk have any reason to want you dead?" the sheriff asked her.

"He's not happy with me or the mandatory domestic violence program he was court-instructed to take. He believes I'm trying to destroy his relationship with his girlfriend. But is that enough to want to kill me?"

She couldn't think of any reason that anyone in town would have to justify her murder.

"People have killed over less," Nash said.

"And killing for love ranks high as a motive. Even if Todd Burk is responsible, our hands are tied without evidence."

"If I have to choose between that man," Nash said, pointing at her assailant, "doing jail time and the one who took out the contract, then I choose the latter. Without the deal, he won't talk. He will probably never make it out of county lockup alive if he's telling the truth. And you'll still be in danger."

The idea of letting that monster, who had most assuredly killed others, walk away scot-free made her want to retch. "This isn't right. At least try to question Burk."

"The second we do," the sheriff said, "it tips our hand, letting him know the contract killer failed and is in our custody. If it is him, that might spur

Burk to hire a replacement to finish the job that much sooner."

Her stomach pitched and rolled. Bile rose in Lynn's throat.

Nash came to her side, putting an arm around her. "I won't gamble with your life." His voice was rough and raw. "We need to get the DA in here to talk."

The sheriff put his hands in his pockets. "You know blanket immunity might not be our only option."

"What are you thinking?" Nash asked.

"That fellow wants to live. Which means getting him released. I say we get immunity only for the charge of attempted murder. Then we let him give us enough rope to hang him on something else before he leaves the state."

"The execution of that idea might be tricky." Nash's jaw clenched. "But it could work."

Chapter Nineteen

What had he been thinking to mouth off at the sheriff like that?

Holden tended to be self-critical, but he also recognized when he had hit a home run. Lately, he had been striking out. All the time.

Tightening his hands on the steering wheel, Holden continued to berate himself. Something that had been made all the easier to do after he went back to Judge Don Rumpke, with hat in hand, and more or less said *pretty please with sugar on top*.

It had definitely been more, not less.

Gritting his teeth, Holden grumbled.

"Everything all right?" Mitch asked from the passenger's seat while eyeing him.

"Yeah. Everything's peachy." His behavior earlier had not been the right approach to bolster the sheriff's confidence in his judgment. Next week, Daniel was leaving town on vacation through the new year. The sheriff was trusting Holden enough to put him in charge. And he almost ruined it. A demotion would be the straw that broke the camel's back. More humiliation than Holden could bear.

He slapped the steering wheel.

"If this is peachy, I'd hate to see lousy," Mitch said.

"I'm upset we weren't able to turn up anything on that contract killer's identity and had to hand it off to the FBI." Once the sheriff's office had turned up nothing it was passed on to Agent Hammond. Twenty-one states currently allowed federal agencies such as the FBI to run searches of driver's license and identification photo databases. "I prefer it when we can take care of it ourselves."

"Yeah, sure. Whatever you say."

Holden pulled up to the Crombie place and parked. The vehicle following with Livingston and Russo did likewise.

They got out of the SUV and met up with the others.

Holden slipped on his cowboy hat. "Do you see that?" He gestured to the front of the house.

"What are we looking at?" Livingston asked.

"That cleared path from the door and down the stairs," Holden said, watching as someone drew all the curtains in the front windows. "Same with the driveway. The Crombies are in their seventies and George has problems with his back. I don't reckon either of them shoveled that snow. But someone did."

The four of them made their way up the stairs to the porch. A scuttling sound came from inside as if one or two individuals were moving in a hurry.

Before knocking, he turned to deputy Ashley Russo. "When I give you the signal, I want you to take Mrs. Crombie to the kitchen. Keep her there and out of the way." He chose Russo because Shirley was capable of accusing a male officer of inappropriate contact if left alone with no witnesses. Hell, she might do the same with Russo, but Holden figured the odds were substantially lower. "If she loses it, goes for a knife or a frying pan or something, put her in cuffs."

"You think it'll come to that?" she asked.

With Shirley Crombie it was best to expect the unexpected. "Never know. Be prepared."

She gave a curt nod. "Got it."

Holden opened the screen door and banged his fist on the main one with authority. The pounding made it clear they were not there to ask a few questions. "Laramie County Sheriff's Department! Open up!" They waited. Thirty seconds ticked by. He banged again. "If you don't open the door, I'll be forced to kick it in!"

More shuffling inside.

The door swung open. Shirley Crombie stood, wearing a seersucker housedress that harkened from the 1960s along with slippers, blocking the entryway. Her wide-eyed gaze washed over the cluster of deputies. Anxiety coated her like sweat. "What do you want?"

Holden held up the official document. "We have a warrant to search the premises." He handed it over and shoved past her, entering the house before she could protest. The deputies followed.

The last one in was Russo. She spotted a shot-gun near the doorjamb and snatched it.

Inside there was only dim natural light that fil-tered in through the curtains.

"Get out of my house," Mrs. Crombie snapped. "You-you-you can't do this."

Holden leveled his gaze at her. "That document you're holding states we can."

Mrs. Crombie tore up the warrant and threw the pieces at him. "Get. Out." She pointed to the front door.

Holden made eye contact with Russo, gave her a slight nod and hiked his thumb in what he pre-sumed was the direction of the kitchen.

Holding the shotgun upright by the barrel, the deputy turned to the older woman. "Mrs. Crom-bie, I need you to come with me," she said in a firm voice. She extended her other arm and eased forward in a way that forced Shirley to move.

"I want my lawyer," Mrs. Crombie said.

Russo kept walking with her arm extended, herding the woman out of the way. "That's fine, ma'am. Call him from the kitchen."

"I—I—I got to get his number," Mrs. Crombie said. "It's upstairs."

Russo didn't hesitate. "Then the call will have to wait, ma'am."

"No! You can't do this."

"It's legal." The deputy didn't back down, making Holden proud. "Take it up with your lawyer. Later."

Once Mrs. Crombie was sequestered in the kitchen, Holden exhaled.

"Where do you want us to start?" Mitch asked.

Holden guessed it would be upstairs since Mrs. Crombie was so hot to get up there, but they had an attic and bedrooms and no telling what else.

So he said, "In here." Crossing the foyer, he looked around.

The house had seen better days. Wallpaper was peeling, dust covered knickknacks, and the floor looked as if it could use a good scrubbing.

In the sitting room, Holden found Mr. Crombie watching television. There were rumors that there was no love lost between George Crombie and Phil Pace. It was time to see if that was true.

He stepped in front of the TV and captured the man's gaze. "Did you hear all that? Do you understand why we're here?"

The gray-haired man nodded. His eyes solemn, his posture hunched.

"I need Phil," Holden said. "Then we can leave you be. We know he's here."

Mr. Crombie's gaze fell, and his mouth twisted like he was chewing on something.

Holden took a knee, forcing the other man to meet his eyes. "I hate interrupting your programs. I know how much you enjoy watching your shows. The sooner we find Phil, the sooner we can be out of your hair. But we're not leaving until we have him. Even if that means we have to pull up every floorboard to find him," Holden said, and Mr. Crombie started wringing his hands. "It's probably difficult dealing with Shirley *and* Phil every day. We can take one burden away for you. Where is he?"

George Crombie adjusted his glasses and looked up at the ceiling. Then met Holden's gaze again.

"He's upstairs." A statement, not a question. It was as Holden suspected.

A nod.

"Which room?"

"Master." Crombie's voice was low, weary. "False wall in the closet."

"Is he armed?" Holden asked.

"Rushing, he forgot to take it." Crombie pointed to a 9mm on the end table next to the remote.

Holden looked at the other two deputies in the room. "Search a secondary bedroom first. So it's not too obvious. Go, get him. Be careful." They nodded in response and left the room, heading up the stairs. He turned back to Mr. Crombie. "Does Phil have a laptop and printer here?"

"Laptop." He gestured to the dining room table across the hall. "No printer."

"Maybe he has one at his apartment that he's been using. Has he left the house since the bench warrant was issued?"

"He was hiding somewhere else the first week.

Don't know where. Then he came here. Hasn't left since."

"Not at all? Not to get food or beer or cigarettes?"

"Shirley wouldn't allow it. Too afraid he'd get caught. She goes shopping once a week. Gets what he needs."

"Do you know if Phil has been writing any harassing letters to Dr. Delgado? Maybe Shirley has been getting them printed and mailing them for him."

The old man's eyes turned glassy with tears. "Phil has done enough to Dr. Delgado. He's not interested in doing anything else."

"Are you okay?" Holden asked. "What did Phil do?"

"That no-good boy got my son killed."

"What do you mean?"

Mr. Crombie pinched his lips together, his gaze lifting across the house. Toward the kitchen.

Holden looked in the same direction. His wife wasn't in sight at that moment. Deputy Russo had probably gotten her to take a seat. "You can tell me," Holden said, his tone gentle yet coaxing. "How did he get Andy killed?"

"Phil was angry at Dr. Delgado because she wouldn't let him shirk his responsibility to attend those classes. He set Andy against her. Poured poisoned words into his ears. Later I found out that he'd taken Andy's medicine. Convinced him that he didn't need those pills. But the doctor had said it was important he took 'em and didn't go off his meds. That rotten boy, Phil, was such a coward. He turned my son into a weapon. To hurt the doctor. Rotten. No-good." Tears leaked from his eyes. "My only son. Dead."

"I'm so sorry." Holden put a hand on his arm.

Scuffling and shouting came from upstairs. Something was knocked over. Glass broke.

"Don't hurt him!" Mrs. Crombie said from the kitchen. "Please, don't hurt him."

"George," Holden said in a softer voice, "would you be willing to make an official statement regarding what you told me? If you did, we could charge him. What Phil did is a crime."

The deputies hauled Phil down the stairs in handcuffs. He was kicking and struggling.

"Mama! Don't let them take me, Mama!"

Mrs. Crombie was doing her darnedest to get out of the kitchen, and Russo showed true grit blocking her. "Don't worry, baby. I'll call the lawyer. Mama will fix this." Then she shrieked foul words at the deputy. Had the nerve to spit in her face.

But Russo handled it with impeccable decorum, not letting the woman pass.

"I can't," George said, his voice a hoarse whisper.

"Why not? We can make him pay for what he did."

"Because..." George stared across the house at

Shirley, who was ranting and raving about injustice in between her bouts of screaming like a banshee. "I've got to live with that. Besides, it won't bring my boy back. Nothing will."

Holden was sorry for the old man. Truly, he was.

But if Phil hadn't written the letters to Lynn, then who did?

Was this all connected to Todd Burk after all?

"I'M NOT SURE about this plan," Deputy District Attorney Melanie Merritt said, sitting in a chair in the sheriff's office. She wore a pantsuit and snow boots. With her intelligent eyes and severe bun, she looked as though she deserved her reputation as a shark in the courtroom.

"If we don't do this," Nash said, "then we can't neutralize the threat. Lynn will still be in danger."

"I understand that. I do. But a bird in the hand is worth more than two in the bush," Melanie said. "Even if the evidence turns out to be irrefutable as you say, you're asking me to give up a contract killer in exchange for what? Potentially a gang member?"

"I'm sorry if 'Contract Killer Apprehended' works better in the headlines, but the fact remains that someone hired him." Nash folded his arms, ensuring his face and tone remained neutral despite his mounting frustration. "We need to know who it is."

Lynn sat in the other chair with a look of disgust on her face.

"Let's call a spade a spade," the sheriff said, seated behind his desk. "This is political. You're thinking about what's going to look better for your career."

"I'm doing my job, considering this as my boss would and how it will affect his career. Not mine." Melanie crossed her legs. "When we're finished here, I have to go to his home, brief him, and convince him whether or not to do this. And yes, the DA is elected just as you are, Sheriff. Oh, wait, you were appointed because of the scandal and haven't faced the blistering heat of an election yet, so please spare me your self-righteousness."

"We're talking about a woman's life here," Nash said. "Her life." Everyone in the room looked at Lynn. "If our plan works, you'll have whoever hired the contractor and the killer. That's a double win. Worst case the DA gets one. This must be worth the risk to your boss."

Uncertainty hung heavy as a curtain on Melanie's face.

"This is the right call," Daniel said. "You have to persuade him. Heaven forbid that something happens to Lynn. Then the headline will read 'DA's Dereliction of Duty Results in Death.'"

"Nice alliteration." Nash nodded. "Readers and voters would eat it up. Bet the headline would sell a lot of newspapers."

Not so easily manipulated, Melanie folded her

hands in her lap, looking unflappable. "I need to be one hundred percent about the best course of action when I speak to the DA. I'm not there yet. From everything I've heard about this contractor, he's clever. He might accept an immunity deal that's less than blanket, but he will most assuredly want it to cover any murders he has committed. Right now, I don't see how he doesn't walk."

A groan rumbled up Nash's throat as his cell phone rang. Taking it from his pocket, he spotted Holden and several other deputies hauling in who he presumed was Phil Pace. Nash glanced at his screen and answered. "Becca, I'm going to put you on speaker. I'm here with the sheriff, the deputy district attorney Melanie Merritt and Lynn." He hit the icon so everyone would be on the same page. "Please tell me we know who this guy is."

"Sorry. We don't."

"We didn't get any hits from the DMV?" Nash asked.

"That's the problem. We got three. All in different states with different names. Same picture. Same man."

"It's the sheriff speaking. One of them must be his real identity."

"That's what I thought, too," Becca said. "But when I dug into each background, I found deceased people."

"Are you sure?" Melanie asked.

"Of course. I wouldn't report it unless I was certain."

Nash swore under his breath. "We needed this."

Smiling, Melanie uncrossed her legs and scooted to the edge of her seat. "Actually, we don't. This works to our benefit."

"How?" Lynn asked, speaking for the first time since they entered the sheriff's office.

"Previously, we were hoping that our contractor would let something slip about another crime he committed. Some other murder so he would do jail time for it. I say we offer an immunity deal. Not blanket. But one that covers any murders, excluding those related to TRK, in case we're wrong on that front."

"Then what do they arrest him on?" Lynn asked.

"Fraud. In the application for a license."

"But that's only a Class 1 misdemeanor," the sheriff said.

"Correct." Melanie's smile widened. "Unless the license was used with the intent to purchase a firearm or used as proof of residency. Then it becomes a Class 4 felony, punishable by up to ten years in prison. For each act. We're talking about thirty years. If he did use it to buy a gun, then we're talking additional charges. Class 6 felony. This will be a federal case. A big one."

Nash let out a little breath of relief. "Becca, I need you to—"

"I know. Verify he's purchased weapons under

the assumed names. Then I'll check to see if there are residences in each state also under those names, because it never hurts to double down."

"Thank you," Nash said.

"No problem. I'm on it." Becca disconnected.

Standing, Melanie straightened her suit jacket. "Now I'm a hundred percent certain the DA will agree to this. It'll take some time to draw up the paperwork."

"How much?" Nash asked.

"A few hours. But I'll need his name. His real name for the document to be legal."

"He may want a personal assurance from you." Unfolding his arms, Nash stepped toward the door and opened it. "That the DA's office is on board with giving him immunity."

"I'd be happy to give it," Melanie said.

She followed him to the interrogation room, where they had him chained and waiting. He stepped inside and she was right behind him.

"This is the deputy district attorney, Melanie Merritt."

Narrowing his eyes, the contractor looked her over. "I'm not important enough to warrant the attention of the DA? All I get is the deputy?"

"I'm the DA's right-hand person. I've given Agent Garner and Sheriff Clark my assurance that you'll have your immunity deal. My next stop is the DA's house to update him. Then I'll get the deal written up. To do so, I'll need your legal name."

"I'll tell you my name, but if you don't hold up your end of the bargain and bring me a deal, remember that pretty little Lynn will pay the price. Because I won't tell you who hired me."

The words made Nash's gut burn.

"You'll have a deal," Melanie said. "I give you my word."

"She needs your name," Nash reminded him.

"Ian. Ellis." He also gave them his Social Security number.

"I'll be back in a few hours." Melanie turned and stepped into the hall.

With one last glance at the man, at Ian, Nash left, shutting the door behind him.

He walked her down the corridor. "Please try to hurry."

"I will."

"And when you're writing up the deal, keep in mind that he's going to look for loopholes."

"Do you know what the biggest part of my job is?"

"Going to trial and getting convictions?"

"No," she said, shaking her head with a smirk. "It's getting criminals to take undesirable plea deals. Bargaining. Ninety percent of cases don't make it to trial. Don't worry, I'm very good at what I do. The deal will be extremely attractive. An offer he won't refuse. But in the end, we're going to send that man to prison for a very long time."

Chapter Twenty

The sun had set, and night had fallen. Pacing in Holden's office, Lynn wished she had something to do other than wait. Melanie was out writing up the immunity deal. The sheriff was taking care of other things in town. It wasn't as if everything in Laramie revolved around her. Becca had gotten proof of the firearm purchases under the aliases and was tracking down evidence of the residencies next.

Nash was on the phone. He'd gotten as far as he could online, digging into Ian Ellis. Now he was making some calls.

She had no idea to whom and quite frankly, didn't care. All she wanted to know was the name of the person who wanted her dead.

Holden came in. "Hey, Lynn, how are you holding up?"

"I need this to be done. Until then?" She shook her head, not knowing the answer. "Did you find out if Phil was responsible for sending the letters?"

Hanging up the phone, Nash stood and joined them.

"Phil isn't behind the letters," Holden said. "We confiscated and searched his laptop to be sure."

They still had no clue who had been harassing her through the mail. Suddenly light-headed, she became unsteady on her feet.

"Sit down." Nash guided her to a chair. "Try to stay off the leg."

"I spoke to George Crombie." Holden leaned against the edge of his desk. "Apparently, Phil instigated what happened to you that night at Turning Point. He took Andy's medication and convinced him you were the devil. George said that he turned his son into a weapon. To hurt you."

"What? How could he? Being off his medication would have caused Andy to suffer a relapse of his symptoms. Delusions. Paranoia. Hallucinations." Recalling how Andy had looked and sounded that night, Lynn pressed a palm to her forehead. "It would explain why he appeared ill." Pale. Sweaty. The tremors. "His aggressive behavior. Especially if he had been led to believe that I was the problem."

How could Phil have been so petty, so manipulative? So cruel to his own brother?

Nash knelt in front of her and held her other hand. "Phil Pace is responsible for Andy's death. Do you hear me?"

She nodded, but she was overwhelmed by sadness. For poor Andy. For Mr. and Mrs. Crombie.

"Some things are beyond our control," Nash continued. "It's time you let this go. It's time to forgive yourself."

"All right," she said sincerely. Maybe it was exhaustion from the past two days. Maybe it was hearing about Phil's culpability. Or maybe she was ready for the first time to finally have the weight lifted.

Letting her eyes close a moment, she took a cleansing breath. "All right." Looking at Nash, she caressed his cheek and kissed him because it would've hurt not to. She loved him so much. "Thank you."

"For what?"

"For being stubborn. For not giving up on us. On me."

"I'll always fight like hell. Remember that."

"I will." She kissed him once more until Holden cleared his throat. Honestly, she'd forgotten he was standing there. "Did you find out anything more about Ian Ellis?" she asked Nash.

"I did after a few calls." He sat in the chair adjacent to hers.

"To who?" Holden asked.

"The Pentagon."

Lynn exchanged a surprised glance with Holden.

"It looks as if Ian was telling the truth," Nash said. "We're the same. In a manner of speaking. He was once in the army. Special Forces. Worked on high-value black ops missions taking out targets."

"But how would Ian know about your background?" Holden asked.

"We weren't together that week he watched me," Lynn said. "Why would he look into you?"

"I've considered that and came up with two possibilities. One, he read that article the paper wrote on you when he was researching how to make it look like TRK was responsible. In it, that journalist mentioned I was your boyfriend."

Her cheeks heated thinking about it. The article had implied that she had been protected by law enforcement because her boyfriend was an FBI agent.

"The other possibility I'm ashamed to admit."

"Why?" Holden asked.

"Because it's possible that he may have seen me watching you."

"Oh." Lynn wasn't sure how she felt about that. "Why were you watching me?"

"I was worried about you. My patience was wearing thin. I went to your house a couple of nights that week. Sat out front. For a while. Debated whether to knock. But never did. That's how I know you had been parking your car in the garage and that he couldn't have marked it there. That it had to have been somewhere else."

"Ian could've thought you two had a lover's spat," Holden said, "but weren't entirely out of the picture. If that's the case, I imagine a good contract killer would thoroughly research all factors."

"Anyway, he was discharged seven years ago. That's when Ian Ellis became a ghost."

Looking out through the window of his office, Holden pushed off his desk and stood. "It's game time."

Lynn turned in her seat. Melanie Merritt was back.

"I should call the sheriff," Holden said. "Let him know."

"Go ahead." Nash marched toward the door. "But we're not waiting on him."

Leaning on her cane, Lynn limped out into the hall.

Melanie held up the document. "The DA has already signed off."

"The verbiage?" Nash asked.

"It's some of my finest work. I'll do the talking in there and I'll get him to sign. I may have to say some tough things, but trust me."

"Okay."

On the way to the interrogation room, Nash ensured Lynn was sitting in the observation room and not putting weight on her injured leg. The wound throbbed, but she was riveted to the scene in the next room.

Melanie slid the deal across the table to Ian Ellis. "All we need is your signature for it to be official."

Ian scrutinized the document, examining every line. "This is not what I asked for. I said immunity from all crimes."

"This is the best deal you're going to get," Melanie said. "You're a contract killer. You have immunity from any homicides you may have committed. Excluding, of course, those of TRK, in case you do turn out to be him."

"I'm not." Ian shook his head.

"Then we don't have a problem," Melanie said.

"But—"

"You want to live, don't you?" Melanie asked.

Ian scoffed at the rhetorical question.

"This offer expires at midnight." Melanie looked at her watch. "Five hours from now." She set down a pen. "After that, you'll be sent to county lockup."

"If you do that, you'll never get the name of who hired me. Lynn Delgado's life will still be in danger."

"That's not my problem," Melanie said without a drop of remorse. "Because it's not the DA's problem."

Nash glanced at Melanie with a look of horror.

"Tell him," she said to Nash. "Our offices have already conferred and after hours of discussion, this is as good as it gets."

Nash lowered his head. "Please. Take this deal. They won't give us anything else."

Melanie set the pen down on top of the document.

Glancing between them, Ian seemed to be weighing his choices. Then he picked up the pen, turned to the last page, and signed.

"Who hired you to kill Lynn?" Nash asked.

"Richard Jennings."

NASH ROCKED BACK on his heels in disbelief. "No." It didn't make any sense. "Rich wouldn't even know how to hire someone like you."

"If that were true, I wouldn't be sitting here."

"How did he find you?" Nash asked.

"Explaining that part is the reason I needed the immunity deal to cover more than the attempted murder of Delgado. I do freelance work for Trident Security," Ian said, and it rang a bell for Nash. "Usually, it entails making problems disappear."

"You mean you've killed people for them," Melanie said.

"When necessary. One of the cofounders, the vice president, Devin Jennings, gave his father my phone number."

The magazine cover flashed through Nash's mind like lightning. "Five Minutes with Devin Jennings: Mitigating Artificial Intelligence Concerns."

"Devin paid for it."

"Cash? Check? Direct deposit?" Melanie asked.

"Same method we've used in the past. Bitcoin."

Nash groaned. Every transaction could be traced on the blockchain, a permanent digital record, linking one address to another. The problem was if someone was transferring money for a nefarious purpose, the address would be anonymous. They would be able to see the money and track it, but not link it to a specific person.

"That better not be your evidence," Melanie said, "or your deal will be null and void."

"I recorded the call, with Richard asking me to kill Lynn Delgado. He insisted that it had to be done before Christmas, and in such a way that would never lead back to him."

That's why Ian tried to make it look like a serial killer was after Lynn.

Melanie folded her hands in front of her. "How do we get our hands on the recording?"

Ian flipped over the document. On the back, he scribbled something. "That's my account and password for Google Drive. There's quite a few video files."

"Related to other murders?" Nash asked.

"Yes."

Melanie stepped closer to the table. "Will any of those files directly link to Trident Security?"

"Some will," Ian said, and Melanie looked like Christmas had come early for the DA's office. "But you should start with the digital file labeled 'Laramie Xmas.' You'll hear everything. Including Rich warning me to watch out for Special Agent Garner. Former ranger. Still in love. Still sniffing around her. There's also copies of texts we exchanged. The last one was after I failed to kill her in the car. He provided me the details of her vacation to the Red Tail Lodge. He was very clear that I wasn't to hurt her friend and to avoid any collateral damage if possible. Lynn was supposed to be the only casualty."

"But why?" Nash asked. "Why on earth would he want her dead?" And why a deadline of Christmas?

Ian shrugged. "I don't ask such things. The why isn't my business. Only the how and when.

If you want to know, you'd have to ask Delgado or Jennings."

Lynn.

Nash spun around and flew out into the hall. By the time he crossed the threshold of the observation room, Lynn was making her way to the door. "What's Rich's reason?"

Her face was pale and shocked. She was shaking her head as if this couldn't be true.

He cupped her arms. "I need you to tell me his reason."

She squeezed her eyes shut. "This all goes back to that night. At Turning Point. With Andy."

"What does Andy Crombie have to do with this? I don't understand."

Lynn looked up at him. Tears glistened in her eyes. "Because of Andy I walked in on Rich. With Cindy Morris. I got the feeling that something inappropriate was going on between them. After I visited my family in Fort Collins and came back to town, I went to see Cindy. She admitted that they had been having an affair."

"So what?"

"He was treating her. She was a client. It was unethical and illegal. But it also got me thinking."

"About what?"

"Whether he'd done this before. Our offices are soundproofed. He said it was to ensure patient privacy and to limit distractions. But what if he had a different motive?"

To have sex with his clients in the office?

Nash had never thought of Rich as a sleazeball before, and now it was hard to think anything else.

"Talking to some of his previous clients," Lynn said, "another woman admitted that he had started an inappropriate relationship with her. After he began treating her."

"Did you report him?"

"No. That's why I don't understand this. I confronted him, of course. Told him it was unacceptable. I gave him a choice. To retire or to be reported. He agreed to change the status of his license to inactive, which I'm able to track to ensure it never reverted back to active, and when the expiration date came, he was supposed to let it expire."

"Did you give him a deadline of Christmas to retire?"

With a shudder, she nodded. "What he did is considered psychological abuse, even though the sex was consensual. I spared him criminal charges by giving him a choice. I promised him I wouldn't tell anyone and that I'd keep it to myself. Why? Why would he hire that man to kill me?"

Nash brought Lynn into his arms and held her, close and tight. "I don't know. But we're damn well going to find out when we arrest him."

Chapter Twenty-One

The drive to Rich's house was surreal.

A man she had once called a friend and considered to be a mentor had hired a contract killer to murder her. After she had done everything possible not to ruin his reputation while fulfilling her ethical obligations.

The convoy hit the old two-lane bridge that ran over the Laramie River, dragging her from her thoughts. They were close now but had just missed a shortcut. There was a frontage road that provided access to the driveway at the rear of the house, where his garage was located.

The shortcut would've saved them five minutes. It was too late to turn back now.

Nash led the way in his truck. A red-and-blue flashing strobe light sat on the dashboard. Behind them were Holden and Mitch in one vehicle. Livingston and Russo in the other.

Shaken, sick, Lynn wrapped her arms around herself. Even after listening to the audio recording and hearing Rich's voice—irrefutable evidence—she still found it hard to believe.

"Back at the hospital," Nash said, dragging her from her thoughts, "I thought it went without saying that things will be different. That I won't be afraid anymore. Even when it comes to the hard stuff. Like sharing. But I realize now, you need to hear me say it. Your concerns are mine. Any issues we have, we can work through it. We just have to be willing to try."

Time was what he needed. And her love. And her almost dying. But he was finally willing to take down the wall. Permanently.

"You're right. I did need to hear it," she said. "As long as we're open with each other, honest, I can see a future for us." A bright, happy one.

They only had to get to the other side of this dark tunnel first.

Nash and the others pulled into the U-shaped driveway at the front of the house.

"Are you sure you want to come inside?" he asked.

"Yes. I don't want to hear his answer second-hand. I need to see his face when he tries to explain."

Nash put a hand on her knee, giving it a little squeeze. "All right. It goes against protocol to have you in there, but you might be useful in helping to get a full confession out of him for everything. Hopefully, we'll wrap this up, putting an end to it once and for all. Just stay behind me and Holden."

She was glad to have him at her side through this. So she didn't have to face it alone. No matter what, she would always be able to count on him. To have her back. To fight for her.

That kind of certainty and the strength of his love was more than she had ever dreamed of. Neither of them was perfect, each beautifully flawed, but she had discovered that they were perfect together.

Getting out of the truck, Lynn had a sense of conviction and finality.

Walking up the front steps, Nash said, "Rich lied. About selling his house. There's no for-sale sign. That bastard never bothered because he thought you'd be dead by now."

The notion sickened her.

Nash knocked as the others gathered behind them, the red-and-blue flashing lights washing over them.

It didn't take long for Rich to open the door. His startled gaze took them in. "Good evening. Is there something I can do for you?"

"As a matter of fact, there is," Nash said. "May we come inside?"

"Certainly." Rich stepped aside, letting them all in. Then he shut the door. "Is there a case you'd like me to consult on?" He looked at Holden. "Like I did for you yesterday."

"Something like that," Holden said.

"Maybe we should go into the living room and sit down." Rich gestured to the room off the foyer.

"We don't need to go to the trouble." Nash pulled out the arrest warrant and handed it to him.

"What's this?" Rich took his reading glasses

from his pocket and put them on. As he began reading, a frown pulled at his mouth.

"It's a warrant for your arrest," Nash said. "For the attempted murder of Lynn Delgado."

"There must be some mistake," Rich stammered. "I'm a pillar of the community. I would never do such a thing. Where did you get such a preposterous idea?"

"From Ian Ellis." Nash stepped up to Rich. "The contract killer sitting in a holding room in the sheriff's department."

"Well, he must be lying." Rich's cheeks reddened. "For some sick, twisted reason. This is some kind of awful mistake."

Nash shook his head. "The only mistake was the one you made. Trusting a hired killer not to record your phone call. You're going to go to prison."

Rich blanched.

"I heard the call," Lynn said. "Between you and Ellis." Her nerves were rubbed raw, but her voice was solid and strong. "Giving him details about me. My life. Telling him that you wanted me dead before Christmas. We were friends. I helped you. I protected you. Why would you do this?"

Straightening, Rich's entire demeanor changed. Gone was the appearance of an innocent victim. "Why?" There was so much venom laced into that one word. "I am the one who helped you after you moved to town. I took pity on you because of your aunt. Do you think I wanted or needed a partner in my practice? I ensured you had plenty of clients. I was *your* friend. And when Andy came there, dead set on killing you, I put myself between him and you." Rich stabbed the air in her direction. "I got shot, took a bullet," he said, holding up the arm that was in a sling, "trying to protect *you*. How do you repay me? By threatening to ruin me. By forcing me into an early retirement. By stealing my practice!"

Dropping the warrant, Rich lunged at Lynn, going for her throat. Her heart jolted as she stumbled backward.

Nash and Holden grabbed him by the arms, restraining him.

The other deputies closed in around her, forming a barricade of bodies and badges.

Reciting his Miranda rights, Holden removed the sling and handcuffed Rich with his wrists in front of him.

"Hiring Ian Ellis wasn't enough?" Nash asked. "Why did you have to terrorize her with those letters? Do you have any idea how sick it was to torment her with the idea that harm was going to come to her before you sent that killer after her?"

"I don't know what you're talking about." Bewilderment washed over Rich's face. "Why would I send her letters advertising the fact that I intended to kill her? I was desperate. Not daft." Then the contours of his expression slowly shifted, changing as though something had dawned on him.

"You didn't send the letters?" Lynn asked.

"No." His voice dropped to a contemplative whisper. "I didn't." Rich swore under his breath.

"But you know who did, don't you?" Nash asked.

"No," Rich snapped, glaring at him. "I don't."

"Cindy." The name left Lynn's mouth on instinct. "She sent the letters. Didn't she?" Lynn recalled that Cindy was originally from Jackson. She went to visit her family often. It would have been easy for her to make stops on the route and send the letters from various mailboxes.

The hot air in Rich deflated and he crumpled inward on himself. "She joked around with the idea. I told her not to. I warned her not to. She understood how you hurt me. The depths of the betrayal. And she wanted to hurt you back."

"You're still seeing her?" Lynn asked, appalled. "Did she know you were planning to kill me?"

Rich straightened, regaining his vigor. "I shouldn't have intervened that night. I should've let Andy kill you!" he spat.

"Get him out of here and down to the station." Holden handed him over to Livingston and Russo.

The two deputies hauled Rich out the door and loaded him into their vehicle.

Coming to her side, Nash curled a protective

arm around her shoulder. Together, they watched him being driven away.

Nash kissed the top of her head. "He can't hurt you anymore."

"I know." She put her head on his chest. "But I'll feel better once Cindy is brought in."

"Don't worry," Nash said. "We'll get her and prove that she was behind the letters. Justice will be served."

ONCE NASH AND Lynn left the house, Holden tugged on a pair of latex gloves and took out an evidence bag. "Ready to do this?" he asked Mitch.

"Yeah, the sooner we get this done and get out of here, the sooner I can have a beer."

"I'll start down here. You take upstairs. Bag and tag anything that might support the case."

"Okay." Pulling on gloves, Mitch bounded up the stairs.

Heading down the hall, Holden looked in the dining room. Candles were burning. Two dirty napkins were on the table. One had red lipstick smeared on it.

He went deeper into the house. In the kitchen, he spotted two wineglasses on the counter. Neither was empty. Two dirty plates were in the sink.

A cold breeze cut through the room, drawing his attention to the back door. It was cracked. As if someone hadn't shut it all the way, perhaps leaving in a hurry.

Had Cindy Morris been here?

The back light was on. He stepped outside and looked around.

Jennings's Mercedes was parked in front of the garage. Beside it were fresh vehicle tracks. Looked like the doctor's dinner companion skedaddled when they arrived. He followed the tracks away from the house down an incline.

Where did it lead? Was there a side road?

HOLDING THE STEERING wheel with his left hand, Nash reached over and took Lynn's hand with his other one. "You did Rich a favor. I'm sorry he didn't see it that way."

"So am I." She sighed, tightening her fingers around his. "I can't believe Cindy Morris is complicit in all this."

He hated the worry on her face. She needed a break from thinking about it. Needed to focus on happy things to come once they made it to the other side. "After we get Cindy, we'll celebrate."

"That sounds nice. I can't wait."

The material of the road shifted as they hit the bridge. "Do you ever wish I made you laugh more? Or took you dancing?"

"What? Where did that come from?"

Your brother. "Something I've been thinking about."

"If I wanted a comedian, I'd be with one. But dancing sounds good."

"Really?"

"Yeah," she said, her spirits lightening. "We could go to the Stagecoach. They have live music. Or we could do some slow dancing at home."

"Now you're talking." Smiling, he looked over at her.

She leaned in to kiss him. Then her gaze veered. "Nash! Look out!"

High beams flashed in front of them, blinding him.

The truck came out of nowhere, bearing down on them at twice their speed, heading straight for them. Nash swerved to the right to avoid a head-on collision. His only thought was to get away from the danger. In those few split seconds, he hadn't considered the consequences of making such a sharp, sudden turn. The tires skidded, the rear end fishtailing. But it was too late. The other truck smashed into his left side. The jarring *bang* of the impact knocked the breath from him, sending a shock wave through his body as they were rammed into the guardrail.

A piercing scrape of metal on metal wailed in the air.

Then the driver accelerated, adding deliberate force that pushed his truck. The smell of burning rubber filled his nose. He yanked on the wheel, trying to turn them in the opposite direction. But they were pinned between the guardrail and the front end of the other truck.

Slamming on the brakes, he hoped that might stop them from being shoved sideways.

Steel whined and screeched. His door groaned as it was crushed inward. The old guardrail on Lynn's side buckled and snapped, giving way.

On pure instinct, he thrust his right arm out over Lynn to protect her from the inevitable fall. He braced himself for the impact.

She screamed, frantic. Her face pale with terror. There was nothing Nash could do to stop them from sliding as they were thrust over the edge. The grille of the other vehicle was locked to his door, dragging it with them. His truck tipped onto the right side and plummeted straight down, crashing into the Laramie River.

A gunshot sound followed as the airbags deployed. The impact sent a horrendous jolt through his body, the seat belt tightening, digging into his flesh. Lynn's screams stopped.

It felt as if somebody had slapped his face as hard as they could. Chalky dust clogged the air.

While the bags deflated, he noticed the windshield was cracked.

Gravity had separated the vehicles. The other truck had flipped and rolled away from them.

His truck was stuck at an awkward angle. Lynn's door was pressed against the river floor. His side was turned up, skyward, but this section of the river was deep enough to cover the truck with water.

"Lynn, can you move?"

She was dazed. Until the icy water flooding into the cabin sharpened her senses, soaking her right side. "Oh God."

Nash released his seat belt and eased down to help her. She screamed as the water rose, closing her mouth just before it covered her head.

He depressed the button on her seat belt, freeing her. Scooping her up, he lifted her from the water. Tilting his head back, he looked at his door. It was the fastest way out. He flipped the switch, unlocking the door, and pulled on the handle as he pushed up. Metal groaned, sticking together. Pain ripped through his wounded biceps. Frigid water rushed up their legs to their waists. He tugged harder, but it wouldn't budge.

The door was jammed shut.

Keep calm. Succumb to panic, you'll never get out.

His gaze fell to the webbed cracks in the windshield. He had to break through it.

Drawing his weapon, he took aim. Pumped three bullets into various spots in the windshield to weaken the glass. The holes poured more water inside, flooding the cabin faster.

Lynn was panting. Soon she'd hyperventilate if she didn't control her breathing. She stared at him with eyes filled with fear.

Desperation to keep her safe overwhelmed everything else. He kicked at the windshield, over and over. Bashing at it, he threw his weight behind every thrust. The water had reached Lynn's neck.

"After everything we've already been through," she said, wet and shivering, "we're going to drown in here."

Like hell they were. "No, we're not." Another kick with his boot heel and the windshield popped out.

Grasping Lynn by her waist, he guided her through the opening first. She swam out and up. He was right behind her. They didn't have far to go to reach the surface.

They popped out of the water. Both of them drawing in a lungful of air. Red-and-blue flashing lights caught his eye. Holden was there. He was climbing down the embankment, and they began swimming toward him.

Seeing that they were all right, Holden took off toward the other vehicle. The rear end of truck was in the water. The front end had managed to hit a tree on land.

Pain radiated through his bad arm with every stroke he took with it.

By the time they had made it to the bank, Mitch was waiting for them with wool blankets.

Nash helped Lynn out of the water, bearing her weight because of her bad leg as they made their way up on to land. He sat her down.

"Are you two okay?" Mitch asked, wrapping a blanket around Lynn.

Teeth chattering, shivering down to the bone, Nash nodded, taking the other blanket and throwing it around himself. "How...did you know?" he asked between sharp breaths. "To come?"

"Holden was following a hunch," Mitch said. "He realized someone else had been at the house. They left when we arrived, taking a back road."

"The sh-sh-shortc-c-cut," Lynn said, trembling, her hair plastered to her head.

Holden jogged back over to them. "The driver is dead. Broken neck from the crash. It was Cindy Morris."

Lynn lowered her head, her shoulders slumping. Another life lost in this madness.

"That could've been us," she said in a low voice. "Necks broken. Or drowned. I hate how close I've come to losing you."

Nash put an arm around her, relieved the circle was now closed and there was no one else to worry about. She leaned into him, resting her head on his shoulder.

"Rich is going to get what he deserves for setting all this in motion," Nash said. "Ian Ellis will go to prison for a long time. And even Rich's son will have his day in court. Melanie will see to it that Trident Security doesn't get away with the things they've done. You're safe. No one is going to hurt you ever again." He'd make sure of it.

"I want to put all of this behind us. No more darkness and death."

He couldn't agree more. This nightmare was over. Once and for all.

And he was ready to focus on the future right now. "Move in with me," Nash blurted out.

Sitting upright, she stared at him. "Did you hit your head in the crash?"

Laughing as his jaw trembled from the cold, he rose to his feet. Then he reached out for her. She took his hand and he pulled her up, facing him. "I didn't hit my head. I know what I want, and that's you, Lola. I'm in this for the long haul."

"You realize part of that haul will be the occasional family dinner in Fort Collins."

More Jake. Wonderful. Nash wasn't going to jump for joy about that, but he was willing to jump through any hoops for her. "I do. And it also means you have to meet my brothers."

They checked in on each other over the phone, but it had been some time since they'd seen one another. It was long overdue, and he couldn't think of a better reason than to introduce the woman he loved.

He stepped closer, erasing the gap between them, letting her lean on him. Regardless of what trials and tribulations might be ahead of them, he wanted to be there to support her. To love her.

She searched his eyes. "You're serious."

"I've never been more so in my life." Lowering his mouth to hers, he kissed her. Through the cold wetness of their skin, their love burned, warming him from the inside out. "Provided you think you can handle having me around all the time," he said.

"I can definitely handle you."

For better or worse, she certainly could.

After they moved in together, he'd make sure she was happy and ready for the next step. Then he'd propose. The two of them being together was right. She was his forever.

"We need to get out of these clothes and warm up." Lynn smiled at him. "Take me home. *Our* home."

* * * * *

Get 4 FREE REWARDS!

We'll send you 2 FREE Books plus 2 FREE Mystery Gifts.

Both the **Harlequin Intrigue®** and **Harlequin®** Romantic Suspense series feature compelling novels filled with heart-racing action-packed romance that will keep you on the edge of your seat.

YES! Please send me 2 FREE novels from the Harlequin Intrigue or Harlequin Romantic Suspense series and my 2 FREE gifts (gifts are worth about $10 retail). After receiving them, if I don't wish to receive any more books, I can return the shipping statement marked "cancel." If I don't cancel, I will receive 6 brand-new Harlequin Intrigue Larger-Print books every month and be billed just $6.24 each in the U.S. or $6.74 each in Canada, a savings of at least 14% off the cover price or 4 brand-new Harlequin Romantic Suspense books every month and be billed just $5.24 each in the U.S. or $5.99 each in Canada, a savings of at least 13% off the cover price. It's quite a bargain! Shipping and handling is just 50¢ per book in the U.S. and $1.25 per book in Canada.* I understand that accepting the 2 free books and gifts places me under no obligation to buy anything. I can always return a shipment and cancel at any time by calling the number below. The free books and gifts are mine to keep no matter what I decide.

Choose one: ☐ **Harlequin Intrigue**
Larger-Print
(199/399 HDN GRA2)

☐ **Harlequin Romantic Suspense**
(240/340 HDN GRCE)

Name (please print)

Address   Apt. #

City   State/Province   Zip/Postal Code

Email: Please check this box ☐ if you would like to receive newsletters and promotional emails from Harlequin Enterprises ULC and its affiliates. You can unsubscribe anytime.

Mail to the **Harlequin Reader Service:**
IN U.S.A.: P.O. Box 1341, Buffalo, NY 14240-8531
IN CANADA: P.O. Box 603, Fort Erie, Ontario L2A 5X3

Want to try 2 free books from another series! Call 1-800-873-8635 or visit www.ReaderService.com.

COUNTRY LEGACY COLLECTION

EMMETT
Diana Palmer

COURTED BY THE COWBOY

THE RANCHER AND THE BABY

Cowboys, adventure and romance await you in this new collection! Enjoy superb reading all year long with books by bestselling authors like Diana Palmer, Sasha Summers and Marie Ferrarella!

YES! Please send me the **Country Legacy Collection**! This collection begins with 3 FREE books and 2 FREE gifts in the first shipment. Along with my 3 free books, I'll also get 3 more books from the **Country Legacy Collection**, which I may either return and owe nothing or keep for the low price of $24.60 U.S./$28.12 CDN each plus $2.99 U.S./$7.49 CDN for shipping and handling per shipment*. If I decide to continue, about once a month for 8 months, I will get 6 or 7 more books but will only pay for 4. That means 2 or 3 books in every shipment will be FREE! If I decide to keep the entire collection, I'll have paid for only 32 books because 19 are FREE! I understand that accepting the 3 free books and gifts places me under no obligation to buy anything. I can always return a shipment and cancel at any time. My free books and gifts are mine to keep no matter what I decide.

☐ 275 HCK 1939   ☐ 475 HCK 1939

Name (please print)

Address   Apt. #

City   State/Province   Zip/Postal Code

Mail to the Harlequin Reader Service:
IN U.S.A.: P.O. Box 1341, Buffalo, NY 14240-8571
IN CANADA: P.O. Box 603, Fort Erie, Ontario L2A 5X3